T0128710

Under the
Willow

The Legend Willie Cane

EDDIE J. CARR

authorHOUSE®

AuthorHouse™
1663 Liberty Drive
Bloomington, IN 47403
www.authorhouse.com
Phone: 1 (800) 839-8640

Published by AuthorHouse 12/19/2016

ISBN: 978-1-5246-5578-5 (sc)
ISBN: 978-1-5246-5577-8 (e)

Library of Congress Control Number: 2016920946

Print information available on the last page.

Contents

Dedicated to

Allen Bruce Aaron
1952-2016

Long time memories of a short time friend.

Chapter 1

SWAMP CHILD

Walter took the pelts from the boat and slowly walked up the embankment towards the cabin. It had been a cool day and he'd done well bagging six beavers and three foxes in his snares. It was a hard living trapping for furs in the Tensaw River Delta. His cabin was about six miles from the community of Stockton, Alabama, and sat about two hundred yards from the Tensaw River. It was built up off of the ground for when the river would rise. Walter built the cabin himself and placed it where the water had never reached his door steps, but it sure come close a couple of times.

The town of Stockton was known more for the shipping of cotton and timber than it was for fur trade but being one of a few trappers in the area, Walter Cane made a living at it. He had learned the trade from his uncle, Wilson Cane. Walter's dad, Riley Cane, was killed in the last known major battle of the civil war at Fort Blakely in April, 1865. Blakely was about twenty miles from Walter's cabin. Being born in April 1858, Walter was just over seven years old when he

1

got the news of his father's death. From that moment on, he learned trapping and fishing from his Uncle Wilson and was now hoping to have a son of his own to pass his skills too.

Walter was thirty four years old. He was around 5'9" and probably weighed a little more than he should have. He had dark brown hair and eyes, his face was worn from days of working in the wind and sun. His hands were callused and he had plenty of scars from his work. His wife Janine was thirty. She too had labored in the life of living in the swamp but had kept her beauty. Janine had long black hair and dark eyes. She was a hard worker and knew what Walter and she needed to survive. They had tried for years to have children, but for some reason God had held off letting them have any, that was, until now. Janine was expecting their first child, and the time had come for them to meet their new addition.

It was October, 1892, and Walter finished cleaning his catch then went in the cabin as the sun fell behind the cypress. The night brought on the sounds of the owls screeching in the swamp along with other sounds of animals and insects, making it an eerie place after the sun went down. He was met by the local midwife Claire Hooper as she was taking a pan of hot water from the stove.

"Your supper is on the stove Walter," she explained. "Janine is having some pains so it won't be long now I am sure. You get you some rest because I may need your help after a while."

Walter nodded and grabbed a plate of stew from the pot hanging over the fire. Claire was a fine woman and everyone knew if you needed tending too, she would come a running. She had no training, but she knew what she was doing and he felt comfortable with her tending to Janine. He got cleaned up and walked into the room to check on Janine. She was in pain but her beauty was still there to see. He took her hand and leaned over kissing her on the head.

"Everything will be alright," Walter told her, "I will be right outside the door and Mrs. Hooper will let me know if she needs me."

Janine half smiled and then grimaced as a pain struck her. After a minute the pain subsided and she looked at Walter.

"He is going to be a legend in this swamp Walter," said Janine, "he has to be. He is tough already."

Not wanting to see her in pain, Walter excused himself and went out and sat down at the table. It was a long night and he laid his head on his arm and fell asleep. He woke several times during the night listening to hear Janine moan and see Mrs. Hooper coming in and out of the bedroom. He stoked the fire and kept hot water ready--the only way he knew to help. It was cold outside and he needed to keep the cabin as warm as possible to keep the dampness out. The dampness was the one bad thing about the swamp, especially in the winter. It wasn't as cold as up north but the dampness made it seem that way. A couple of hours before dawn, Walter sat in the rocking chair and leaned his head back and fell asleep.

The morning sun coming through the window woke him and he sat forward. He looked out the window and could see the frost thick on the ground. He stood and walked to the stove placing more wood inside it then he placed more wood in the fireplace. Walter poured himself a cup of coffee sat down at the table. There were no sounds coming from the bedroom and he thought that Janine had finally fallen asleep. After about ten minutes, the door to the bedroom opened and Mrs. Hooper came emerged from the bedroom, smiling.

"Walter," she said, "Janine is doing fine and I believe this is what you and she wanted, a nice, healthy, baby boy." "Here you are Walter," she said, as she handed him a blanket with his son wrapped inside.

A smile crossed Walter's lips as he took the infant in his arms. The baby had a head of dark hair and dark eyes, just like his mother. He shifted around so that Walter was afraid that he was going to drop the child but he wasn't about to let go.

"You may want to take him to his maw so she can feed him," said Mrs. Hooper, grinning from ear to ear.

"Yes ma'am, I will do that right now," Walter agreed.

Walter entered the bedroom and saw Janine half sitting in the bed. She had had a long night and he knew she was tired, yet his heart was warmed when he saw her smiling at him. He walked over to her leaned over and kissed her. He then handed her the baby.

"He has your hair and eyes," Walter said, proudly.

"Yes," Janine said, "but he will be a big one. He may even be bigger than you."

Walter looked at the baby and said, "Could be." "It will be good to have a strong healthy son to help with the chores and trapping. Of course you will have to teach him to read and write because I ain't no good with that, but he will be smart to the ways of the swamp and the world."

"Don't you think we need to let him get a little bigger before we start learning him to trap and such?" Janine asked.

Walter scratched his head and smiled. "Yeah, I guess you are right, we probably need to let him learn to walk, at least before he starts learning."

They both smiled and watched as Janine nursed the child. She was very tired and needed rest. Walter decided to go get some things done around the cabin while she and the child napped. Walter stood and started to the door, there he stopped and looked back at Janine.

"What are we going to name him?" he asked.

"Well," Janine replied, "since all you Cane men seem to start your name with a "W", except for your paw, I think we could call him Willie."

Walter stood in the door pondering the name and nodding to himself. "Yeah, yeah, that sounds like a good name." "Willie Cane, kinda keeps it in the family," Walter said. "Willie Cane!"

He opened the door and met Mrs. Hooper coming in.

"Thank you Mrs. Hooper for your help," Walter said, "as always you are an angel," as he reached over and patted her on the shoulder. "That there is my son Mrs. Hooper, Willie Cane, and you know what?"

"No, what's that Walter?" Claire asked.

"He is going to make a name for himself around here," Walter said, smiling from ear to ear. "He is going to be the best trapper in these parts and everyone is going to know about him before his days are done. Just mark my words Mrs. Hooper, you just mark my words."

Claire was smiling and suggested that Walter go get some sleep and that he may be dreaming too big. They laughed and Walter went out onto the porch. He yelled the name three times as loud as he could.

It was as if he was telling the swamp that his son was coming and that he would rule the swamp before long. "Willie Cane," he yelled as the name echoed off of the trees and embankment across the river. "Willie Cane is here and he will know everything about you. He will know all the animals and all the people around here and he will be known. Willie Cane is my son and he is coming, Willie is coming."

Walter stepped off of the porch and headed towards the lean-to at the rear of the cabin. He grabbed a hoe and headed towards the garden to dig up some sweet potatoes and get some turnips. He had some fresh venison in the meat house and there was going to be a feast for dinner. To say he was happy would not have matched his feelings. He had a son and he was one proud paw. Walter now had the chance to raise and teach his son. He had the opportunity to do something that he never got the chance to have done to him. He would love and cherish his son and teach him how to survive. Janine had given him the most precious gift that any man could receive and he loved her more than ever. Together they would raise the boy to be a man. Together they would raise their son, Willie Cane.

Mrs. Hooper had cooked up a fine meal and they sit at the table eating. "Claire," Walter started, "I want to thank you for your help. I couldn't have made it without you here these last couple of days."

Claire smiled and said; "Wouldn't have missed it for the world. I been doing this for a while and I declare I ain't never heard no carryings' on like what you was a-doin. I was plum proud for you and Mrs. Janine."

Walter reached in his pocket and pulled out fifteen

dollars and slid it across the table to Mrs. Hooper. "You're welcome here anytime," he told her. "You're a good friend."

Claire took the money and put it in her apron pocket. "You know you are welcome Walter" she said. "I'll stay a couple of days till the missy gets on her feet, then I best be getting on back home afore my old man forgets me. I'm goanna take Mrs. Janine some soup, help her get her strength back up. I'll get you some jerky for tomorrow, I figure you'll be going to check your traps in the morning first light."

Walter again thanked her and walked out on the porch to smoke his pipe. All he had left to smoke was some old rabbit tobacco, but it was good in a pinch. He sat in the rocker on the porch and looked down the Tensaw. The moon was as large as he had ever seen it and was shining off the river like a torch. The owls were at it again, but for some reason they sounded a little more active. Even the whip-o-wills was singing like he'd never heard them sing before. Some coyotes yelped off in the distance, but it was so quiet that he swore he could hear the piano from the bars in town every once in a while.

The night was cool as he sat pondering what he would do and how he would raise his son. He had missed growing up with his dad, but he sure didn't want to lose a day teaching Willie. As he sat there he could feel a tightness in his chest and figured he had had too much excitement for one day. He relaxed and sat watching the river flow down toward Mobile Bay. The tightness went away and he went on in the cabin. He had a full day of trapping ahead of him, and after missing a day he may have some full traps. It was hard work but he enjoyed it; it made him a living.

After tomorrow he would take the skins to the general store in Mobile and sell them. He could then get some supplies and buy some bonds that he had been getting for the past couple of years. He didn't know that much about them but Mr. Kennedy at the bank told him they would be worth something one day.

He went in to check on Janine and found all three of them sound asleep. Ms. Hooper was in the rocker getting some well-deserved sleep. Janine was laying on her side with Willie beside her. Walter leaned over and kissed Janine. He reached over and turned down the kerosene lamp, taking some of the brightness out of the room. He then laid some dried skins in front of the fireplace, stoked the fire and laid down on the skins. He lay looking into the fire as it flickered and said a silent prayer, thanking God for his family and friends. Soon his eyes grew heavy and he fell off to sleep.

Chapter 2

BIG CITY ADVENTURE

Ten years had passed since the night Willie had come into the world. He had followed his paw around since he was able to walk and he was a natural. He learned how to trap, hunt, fish and everything that he would need to do to survive. His maw taught him how to read and write and even though he was not an expert, he was able to write letters and read books. He wasn't able to go to the school because it was just too far away in the town of Blakely. He liked meeting people, but living in the swamp made it hard. He had very few friends but did have one in particular. His best friend was a Creek Indian boy known as Sam Calhoun. That was his English name anyway. His Indian name was Little Lizard. Sam was about three years older than Willie but they struck up a friendship at a festival in Stockton.

Willie was about an inch taller than his paw at ten years old and was looking to be several inches taller before he stopped growing. It didn't really matter how much taller he was, he still respected his paw and would not cross him for nothing. If he even thought about doing something that was against his parents teaching, that plum limb would cross his mind and he wanted nothing to do with that. His paw was a strong man and both his maw and paw had got his attention with a limb that just would not break easily. Some folks would have called it cruel, but Willie knew it was teaching him the right and wrong of things. It may have hurt some, but he accepted it as a life lesson and a guideline for doing things the right way. The worse he ever got was when he bogged Flame, the family mule, up to his knees in the marsh. His paw worked a couple of hours getting that mule out without hurting him, then Willie got a lesson in paying attention to what he was told. Flame was the only animal that the Cane's had for transportation and plowing. If they had of lost him, they would have been in a mess. With all that said, Willie learned respect and the meaning of hard work. He grew up in the swamp and learned its ways and how to survive. Willie loved his maw and paw and was grateful for everything they had taught him.

It was February of 1902. Trapping had been pretty good and Walter had a load of furs ready for sale. He contacted Mr. Hastie at the general store in Stockton about the market and was told he could get a real fair price if he took them to Mobile to the trading post there. It was a Thursday morning when Walter started loading up his raft for the trip. Willie wanted to go but didn't think his paw would let him. Willie had never been to a city before and was curious about how big it was. He helped his paw get the raft loaded and all the pelts tied down and then he started back towards the cabin.

Walter yelled, "Willie, go get them lunch buckets your maws got for us and get you a change of clothes. We want be back till late Sunday night, depending on the tide."

Willie ran up that bank fast as he could. Maw was standing in the door with the food and a change of clothes. She was grinning from ear to ear, just like Willie. He grabbed the stuff and turned to run back down to the raft.

He stopped and turned around, "Maw," Willie asked, "what about you?"

Janine smiled, "You run along and help your paw, I will be fine. Keep an eye on him and make sure none of them fancy women flirt with him in that big city. I already been there a couple of times."

"Awe maw," Willie said, "you know paw has the prettiest lady around." He smiled at her and then ran down to the raft, handing his paw the stuff then climbed on. He waved back at his maw as his paw pushed the raft out into the current and slowly started drifting down the Tensaw towards Mobile Bay.

The raft was only about nine feet across and fifteen feet long. Walter had cut pine logs and lashed them together using some strong hemp and large railroad spikes he had gotten from a friend at the train depot. It was sturdy and he added a rudder to help him steer. He had also cornered a nice size piece of canvas to hoist for a sail when the wind was blowing and today there was a breeze out of the northwest that would help them get to Mobile a little quicker. The current was moving around three or four miles an hour, but with the sail the raft would move six or seven miles in an hour. It wasn't fast, but it would get them to Mobile before dark.

Walter worked the raft through the Tensaw and over to Middle River, then cut across the bayou to the faster moving Mobile River. There they passed the first settlement called Twenty-Seven Mile Bluff, the first site of Mobile. Willie had heard they had to move the town because it kept flooding when the river would rise. Now the city settled at the mouth of Mobile Bay and was the entrance to Alabama from the Gulf of Mexico. As they started towards Mobile, Willie laid back on the furs and looked at the beauty of the river banks. Large cedar trees and cypress knees lined the river as moss hung lazily, moving with the breeze. Deer and wild hogs drank from the river and blue heron waded in the shallows seeking minnows or fish they could sneak up on. It was peaceful as Willie listened to sea gulls flying overhead, squalling and searching for something to eat. It was his first trip away from Stockton away from the river swamp and it was more than he had ever dreamed of. The breeze was cool but the sun was warming him and he nodded off to sleep.

Walter walked up and bumped Willie's foot. "Time to get up son, we are here." Willie opened his eyes and stood slowly. The raft had been tied to a pier and a ladder led up to the main level of the huge wharf. Ahead of them were several large ships tied up, some with smoke coming out of large tubes on them. They were bigger than anything Willie had ever laid eyes on, except from a book. Men were working on them, loading and unloading all kinds of things. He followed his paw up the ladder until he reached the top and stepped onto the wharf. He stood looking at the town, buildings taller than he could imagine. Men and women were busily walking around as if they were getting ready for something. Bales of cotton were stacked four and five bales high and there must have been thousands of them.

"Willie," Walter said. "You stay here with the raft while

I go speak to the man at the trading post. I will be back shortly."

"Paw," Willie asked, "why are all these folks in such a hurry?"

"Well, they are getting ready for something they call a parade," Walter said. "Seems they celebrate once a year around here and have some parades. They call it Mardi Gras and from what I hear tell they have a heck of a party round here. Now, you stay put and I'll be back soon."

Willie nodded and sat down on the edge of the wharf. He watched people fishing and just sitting around talking. A dirty looking man came up and sat down beside him.

"What's your name kid?" the stranger asked.

Willie didn't like this man for some reason, but he was taught to respect elder folks. "My name is Willie Cane," he responded.

"Those furs belong to you?" The stranger asked.

"Those furs belong to my paw and he will be back soon," Willie answered. Willie did not want to answer this man. He wanted the stranger to go away but he wouldn't.

"I bet you can get some good money for them," said the stranger.

"I speck so," Willie replied.

"You ain't one much for talking are you kid?" asked the man.

Willie was one that liked to talk some but he didn't have much to say to this fellow.

"Mister," Willie said, "I don't know you and I don't think I want too. If you got questions about these furs, then I suggest you hang around till my paw gets back and I'm sure he can let you know all about them."

Willie had sized the man up and figured he was up to no good. The man was tall, maybe six foot or better and looked as if he had been sleeping in a barn. He smelled bad too, it was sure that he hadn't had a bath or shaved in a while. His clothes fit loose and he had a pistol on his side. It was old looking but Willie was able to see the etching of Colt on the side of it. Willie was just fixing to tell the man he needed to leave when a man riding a horse and dressed in a uniform came riding down the wharf.

The stranger stood up quickly and said, "Talk to you later kid." He then headed in the opposite direction of the uniformed man. Willie just sat there and could hear people talking to the man calling him officer. The officer came up to Willie and looked down on him from the horse.

"How are you today son?" the man asked.

Willie felt more at ease with this man and responded. "Fair, I guess, sir."

"What is your name son?" he asked.

"Willie Cane, sir," Willie answered, "I live up in Stockton, or at least near there. My paw came here to sell some furs."

"Well, my name is Carlton Bridges," the man said. "I am one of the constables around here. If you need any help while you are here, you just yell out." Looking at Willie, Mr. Bridges asked, "Who was that man that was sitting here?"

Willie shrugged his shoulders and said, "I don't know who he was, he just started asking a lot of questions about them furs. He saw you coming and cut a shuck. To tell you the truth sir, I was glad, he seemed a lot strange to me. I will sure be glad when my paw gets back."

Mr. Bridges climbed down from his horse and said,

"Tell you what Willie, I don't have much going on, how about I just sit here with you until he returns?"

"I'd be thankful to you sir," exclaimed Willie.

They sat and talked for a while. Willie was told all about Mardi Gras and things that were going on. Finally Walter returned and talked with the constable for a while. He also had a wagon to load the furs on and take them back to the trading post. Willie had learned at a young age to not butt in on grown folks when they were talking, so he didn't know what his paw and the officer spoke about. He just got busy getting the furs on the wagon.

After the wagon was full, Walter drove the team back to the Trading Post. Willie looked as they traveled down cobble stone streets past large buildings. People were everywhere, some working, some shopping and a few men that looked to be sleeping on the wooden sidewalks. The stores had huge windows in them with all kinds of stuff like dresses, hats, and saddles but the one that caught Willie's eye was the one with the big candy cane in the window. It was as big as any he had ever seen and he imagined that it would take more than a few minutes to gnaw it down. The aroma of food filled the streets and there were signs that said Blue Plate Special-80 cents. Willie wasn't really sure what a blue plate special was, but he figured it had something to do with food.

They came up in front of this large building that had furs stacked up inside. They had all kinds and plenty of them. Willie's paw went inside and came back out with a man wearing a large apron. He counted out a handful of money to Walter and they shook hands. They left the loaded wagon in front of the store, and as they were walking away a couple of men started unloading the wagon. It was late afternoon, so Walter decided to get a room and stay the night. They walked down the street and past a park.

"That there is called Bienville Square, Willie," Walter said. "It was named after some French man that helped settle this town." They came up to the front of the candy store and Walter walked inside. Willie followed and just stood there with his mouth open looking at all the different kinds of candy. "Pick you out something Willie, you have earned it," Walter said.

Willie got some gum balls and a couple of peppermint sticks and was as happy as a squirrel with an acorn. After they left the store, they walked down to a building that read Rooms to Rent. Walter paid a man $1.50 for a room and they went upstairs and into the room. It was up two flights of stairs and when you looked out the window you could see the whole street, all way down to the Trading Post. After washing up, they went down to a place inside the hotel and got some food. The food was either good or Willie was just plain hungry, but it was nowhere close to being as good as Maw's. Looking out the window, Willie could see that the people started gathering on the sidewalks. It looked to be about an hour before dark.

"Come on Willie, you can watch the parade." Walter said.

Willie stepped out and nudged his way to the front of the sidewalk. Walter was only a few steps behind so as to keep an eye on Willie. There was no doubt that Willie was excited.

Willie could hear music and when he looked down the street he saw a band coming and they were a playing up a storm. There were some folks in front and some behind the band dancing in the street and wearing all kinds of mask. They came right in front of Willie and when they passed, there were more behind them. There were these things they called floats that came by with men wearing costumes and masks. The floats were fixed up with all sorts of decorations. People were clapping and yelling. About six of the floats came by and then they were gone, but not the people. They were dancing in the streets and drinking pretty heavily. Walter motioned for Willie to come on and they started walking back towards the hotel.

Willie stopped to watch some kids popping fireworks. Walter had walked on down the street. Willie watched for a few minutes and leaned down and picked up an oak limb that was laying on the ground. He turned and started towards the hotel, not seeing his paw and dragging the limb across the boards on the sidewalk.

As Willie approached an open space between two buildings he heard a voice saying "get your hands up." Now he had herd that voice before and it was from the man that had bothered him back at the wharf. Willie eased to the corner and looked around into the dim alley way. It was the man that had the gun in his belt, but now he had that gun pointed at someone. Willie couldn't see who it was. The stranger had his back to Willie and did not see him. Willie waited and then the man that this stranger had the gun on spoke. "Look I don't have any money on me." Willie knew that voice too, it was his paw.

"Mister, don't make me kill you, I know you sold them furs today, I met your boy at the wharf," the stranger said. "He is pretty smart because he kept telling me you would be back soon." "By the way, where is that kid?"

Walter told the stranger that the money was back in the room and he could follow him if he wanted it. The stranger demanded that Walter give him the money because he knew that it was on him.

The stranger raised the gun and started to aim at Walter when he was struck across the arm. The gun went off, the bullet going harmlessly into the ground while the man grabbed his arm in pain. People began to run towards them, and the officer, Mr. Bridges, ran up and grabbed that stranger before he could take a step.

"What happened here Mr. Cane?" asked Officer Bridges Walter explained that the stranger was trying to take his money and that he had threatened to shoot him. "If not for my son, I think he would have done it."

Officer Bridges told that man he was under arrest and took him away. Willie stood there shaking, still holding that oak limb. His paw walked up to him and hugged him.

Walter didn't know if he ought to whip Willie or chew him out. He also knew that Willie had saved them from losing a good bit of money and possibly his life.

"Son," Walter said, "you could have gotten hurt." "I should whip the fire out of you with that oak limb but I guess I am too proud of you to do that. I don't know what I would have done if something would have happened to you, I sure wouldn't want to face your maw. Anyway it turned out good and the only one hurting is that fellow." Walter hugged Willie again and they headed for the hotel.

In the room Walter sat by the window and looked down onto the street. People were still milling around and there was a buzz about the kid that broke the man's arm with a stick and how he had saved a robbery. Walter thought to himself about how he once yelled to the swamp that Willie would be famous. Seemed that Willie was also going to be known further than the swamp. Smiling, he blew the lamp out and went to bed.

The morning sun came through the window and Willie opened his eyes. About the time he sat up in bed his father came through the door.

"Hurry up, Willie," said Walter, "we have got to get headed back home."

Willie got dressed and Walter walked over to him. He handed Willie a box and said, "You have worked hard son, helping me trap and all so you earned that," pointing to the box.

Willie opened the box and there was the finest bowie knife he had ever seen. It had a scabbard and could hook to his belt. Willie grinned and took the knife quickly hanging it on his belt.

"Thanks Paw, it is the best gift I ever got." Willie said.

"You be careful with it till you learn how to use it better," Walter explained, "It is real sharp. I don't need you cutting yourself."

"I will be careful Paw," said Willie.

"I know you will son, now let's get moving," Walter said, "We need to see what the tide is doing and head on back home."

They gathered up the supplies that Walter had bought and got back to the wharf. They loaded the raft and soon shoved off into the Mobile River. The current wasn't moving at all but there was a light breeze from the gulf and it helped them move north slowly. The tide was called a neap tide. A neap tide was when the water just about stood still, not coming in or going out. On this day it was so still that it was not moving either way. After about an hour the water began to move a little going north which was good because the current would take them towards Stockton. This helped push the raft which was good because the wind had almost stopped. It did take them a little longer to get home. Sometimes they would use push poles to help them move faster but in certain places the river was too deep and they would just have to use what current there was. It was past sundown when they finally reached home. Janine met them as they came up the bank and hugged Willie and Walter.

"Well now, I hope yawl had a good trip and everything went well," Janine said.

Walter looked at Willie then at Janine and said "Let's just say, it was a very eventful trip. I will tell you all about it. We are a little hungry."

Janine smiled at them and said, "Got some supper cooked, figured you would be wanting something to eat. Wash up and I will set the table, then yawl can tell me what happened."

Walter grinned at Willie and said, "Well now that may take us a few minutes but we will try." They laughed and headed towards the cabin.

Chapter 3

STARTING A LEGACY

Two years had passed since that night in Mobile. Willie was about three inches taller and stood about six feet at the age of twelve. He had been working beside with his paw trapping and fishing. He had learned the skill of tracking and was as good as his paw about the animals of the swamp. He knew what they liked to eat and how to catch them. He knew which ones would hurt you and what to do when you caught one. Willie had got to the point that his paw would let him lead hunters through the swamps either to get them to another place they wanted to go or help them sport hunt for deer, bear and hogs.

Sam Calhoun, Willie's friend, came to go with Willie and run some traps up near Fort Mims. It was a place that neither boy wanted to go. Word was that the place was haunted and the woods around it were no fun to be in. Walter was sick and Willie had noticed his paw getting weaker over the past year or so. It was as if Walter was having a hard time breathing sometimes. Willie had seen him grabbing his chest a couple of times. Each time Walter would have to sit down and rest before going on. They had also been going to church a lot more and Walter had joined the church. Seemed as if he was preparing for something. Willie didn't mind going to church and enjoyed learning about the Bible. He also got to make some friends and there were some mighty pretty girls there too, but he was too shy to talk to them. It was strange, but his maw was happy for Walter and Willie to be going to church, so he just relaxed and enjoyed it.

Fort Mims was around seven miles upriver from the cabin, so Sam and Willie started out early in the morning. They stayed close to shore and paddled pretty steady, checking traps along the way. It seemed to be going pretty good as they had four nice beavers, an otter and a big red fox. As they neared Fort Mims, the traps weren't as good to them. They landed the boat and Sam went to check some traps on the east side of the fort. Willie walked north and checked several traps in that area. These woods made him jumpy and he would fuss at himself for letting the tales he heard get under his skin. With nothing to show on the north side of the fort, he walked toward the south. He walked to a clearing and right outside the fort's walls, he stopped dead in his tracks.

He stood looking at the walls. His maw had read stories to him about the massacre that had happened there. This was the first time he had been near the fort without his paw. He didn't like it. He wasn't afraid of much of anything, but this placed spooked him. Fort Mims was actually the home of Samuel Mims, kind of a big plantation looking home. When word got out that the Creek Indians in the area had been attacking folks, a Major Daniel Beasley had gathered up some soldiers and volunteers along with some women and children. They gathered there and built a wall around the place. Story goes that the folks kept waiting for the attack, but it didn't come so they kind of relaxed.

On August 30, 1813, the attack happened in broad daylight. The gates were open, so the Creek Indians, Red Sticks, as they were called, led by William 'Red Eagle' Rutherford, and some other leaders, just came through opened gates. Five hundred or more in the fort were killed and only fifty to one hundred Indians. No one knows exactly, but they do say that most all of the women and children were killed. Since then, this place is said to be holding those that died here. All Willie knew was that it was an eerie place and he didn't care much for it.

He was standing there listening when all of a sudden he heard what he thought was a ghost yelling. He started to high tale it when he heard the yell again. This time he stopped to listen. It came again from the woods. He could hear Sam yelling for him. He started in the direction of the yelling and came to a scattered patch of pines with a small clearing. Sam yelled at Willie to look out and just as he did Willie saw the big boar coming down on him. Willie took off running then jumped high as he could catching a low limb and swinging up just as the boar passed inches under his feet. With those tusk he would have cut Willie open. Willie settled himself on a larger limb and looked over at Sam roosting on a water oak.

"What happened?" Willie ask.

"Beats me," Sam said, "was just fixing to check that trap over there and he came out of the brush, snorting and grunting. I might near didn't make it up this oak. I believe he has a bad tooth or something."

"Why do you say that?" asked Willie.

"Well, something got him all riled up," Sam replied.

That boar kept walking around and grunting, pawing at the ground and squealing. It was late in the day and Willie sat thinking of what they could do. It was certain that the big hog wasn't going anywhere. One thing for sure, Willie did not want to be in the woods after dark, especially in this place. After about twenty minutes Willie looked over at Sam.

"Hey Sam," Willie yelled. When he did that boar spun around and headed for Willie's tree, and stood there under it. He did exactly what Willie expected him to do.

Sam said, "Willie, don't do that man, he may uproot that tree."

Willie looked over at Sam and said, "When I tell you, I want you to yell."

"What are you going to do Willie?" Sam asked, as he noticed Willie taking out his bowie knife.

"Just yell." said Willie. He would have one chance to get this hog. If he missed then he would be in a mess for sure. "Now Sam!"

Sam yelled and that boar turned around. Just as he started to step towards Sam, Willie jumped from the safety of the tree and he landed straddling that boar. The hog leaped forward. As quick as Willie got his balance, he got a grip on that hogs ear. The hog was turning his head back towards Willie. That bowie knife came down and caught the hog right behind the ear and he dropped in his tracks. Willie wanted to be sure so he stuck the hog a couple more times. Willie sat on the ground and looked at Sam climbing down out of the oak.

Willie inspected the hog and stood up. "I'll be darned," he said as he looked at Sam.

"What is it?" asked Sam.

"He did have a bad tooth," exclaimed Willie. "You can clean him."

"Why do I have to clean him?" asked Sam.

"Because I killed him, and if I hadn't, you would still be sitting in that oak eating acorns with the squirrels."

"I could have killed him if I had of wanted to," Sam said.

"Then why didn't you?" asked Willie.

"Willie Cane, you are one crazy man," Sam said. "That there was some kind of grit for any man."

"Sam," Willie said, "I am not a man, I am only twelve."

"Say what you want, not many men would have did what you just done," Sam said. "I damn sure wouldn't have jumped on no wild boar and I wouldn't mess with you either."

"You don't have to worry Sam, you are my friend," Willie said.

"That makes me feel good," Sam said. "Why did you do it?"

Willie looked back at him and smiled. "Because maw is cooking some chicken and dumpling tonight, ain't no hog going to keep me from that," he said. "Now grab that hogs leg and let's get going."

After checking the rest of the traps they loaded the canoe with the hog and three coons and headed home. It was a heck of a day with what they already had trapped.

There would be a lot of skinning to do when they reached the cabin. The current was against them and they would have to paddle hard to get back home before dark.

The old boat was a little heavy with the weight of the hog and other animals. Willie and Sam were struggling against the current and had moved the boat close to shore so that they could use the push poles as much as they could. With a mile or so to go Willie noticed that they had company following them. The big boar that Willie had killed was bleeding a lot and the blood was seeping through the bottom of the boat and leaving a trail of blood in the water. As he looked behind them he noticed a pretty large alligator trailing the boat but, staying back about seventy or eighty feet.

Willie knew that the gator had the taste of blood from the hog and was looking for food. He also knew that if that gator was hungry enough that they may be in trouble because he would come after the meat. The old boat was not in that great a shape and Willie didn't want that gator ramming the boat. Willie kept a watch on the gator and he noticed him getting closer and closer to the boat. All of sudden the gator came out of the water and lunged at the rear of the boat. He was too far back to even be close but he started making a sound that Willie felt sure was to let them know he was the boss. The gator went under and came back up within ten feet of the back of the boat. If that gator charged and came up like he had just done, he would sink the boat.

As long as Willie could see the gator things were fine, and he felt comfortable until that gator went under water. Willie was pushing along the bottom and searching the top of the water for any sign of bubbles. The bubbles would give

Willie some idea of where the gator was under water. Sam hadn't noticed the gator until the noise and then the gator came up about five feet from the bow. That old boat was about twelve foot long and that gator was at least thirteen and looked to weigh around eight or nine hundred pounds. Willie did notice that the gators right rear foot was half gone. It looked as if he had lost it, probably in a fight with another gator that he had apparently won. He only had two toes on the foot.

Sam wasn't at all happy about the situation and started wiggling and moving around in the boat. Willie was amazed at the size of the gator and knew that if the gator was to hit the boat, they would be in trouble.

"Keep pushing Sam," Willie said. "If we stop the boat, he may come after us, he wants something to eat and I don't want it to be us."

Sam didn't say anything, he just picked up the pace as if he was trying to move faster than that gator. Willie cut the front quarter off of that big hog and tied a rope around it. The gator had dropped back a little because Sam was working as hard as he could to get away. Willie dropped the quarter of hog out of the boat and started dragging it behind the boat. That gator picked up his pace as the meat went past him and started closing in on it.

Willie was waiting on him to take the meat. That would be better than taking that gator back to the cabin and skinning him out. Willie had had enough excitement for the day and wanted nothing to do with the big gator. He would save that fight for another day.

The gator caught up to the hog quarter and latched down on it. When he did, Willie cut the rope and let him have the whole thing. Willie grabbed the pole and began helping push the boat along. Soon Willie felt safe and they slowed down a little. The gator took the hog quarter and went under. It was fresh meat and not exactly what the big fellow wanted but it was enough to satisfy him for now. He would take the meat and hide it under a log, let it rot and then come back to eat it later. At least the gator's attention and want had been met and the boys could make it home without being stuck under a log somewhere in the river.

Finally Sam spoke, "Well that was close, and was some sure fire smart thinking on your part. If you hadn't of fed that gator, we might have been supper for sure."

"Ain't no worry for you Sam," Willie said. "Two Toes wanted tender meat and you look a might tuff to chew on."

"You are a smart ass, ain't ya!" Sam said. "A smart ass, but this one time I would have hoped you was right. Where did you come up with "Two Toes"?"

"His back foot didn't have but two toes on it," Willie said, "Didn't you see it?"

Sam looked at Willie and said, "Man, I wasn't looking at that gators foot, I was praying for the Indian god's to help us out. I seen his eyes and it looked to me like he was saying grace."

The boys laughed as they rounded the bend and could see the cabin.

They landed the boat and unloaded all the animals they had snared and killed. Walter came out to meet them and help unload the boat. He looked like he was feeling better and was up and around pretty good. He smiled at the catch and then asked about the hog and why one front shoulder quarter was gone. It didn't take Sam long to explain all the things that had happened on that day and Willie just sat back and let him tell the tales.

After listening to the day's events, Walter smiled at Willie and was thinking about the day he was born. He told the swamp that Willie was coming. He knew it would happen, he just didn't know it would start so early in Willie's life. Willie was on the verge of becoming a man and he already had a man's body. As young as he was he had already seen and done a lot of things.

Walter knew that he would not get to see Willie grow up and become the king of the swamp. According to the doctor in Bay Minette, Walter didn't have much time left. He had some heart problems and there was nothing the doctor could do for him. It wasn't something that Willie needed to know so Walter was just going to keep teaching him and spending what time he had left enjoying his son.

"Okay boys," Walter said, "let's go eat some supper and we will get these critters cleaned and that hog cut up later. I am glad that gator didn't hit that old boat, you fellow's would have sunk sure as I am talking to you."

By the way Walter continued, "Willie, I stopped in and spoke to Mr. Brewer in Bay Minette. He is building us a fine new boat that should be ready next week. We will go and pick it up then. It will be a little wider and two foot longer than the old boat and I don't think "Two Toes" will want to mess with it."

Willie smiled, "That sounds great Paw, be looking forward to getting it."

Willie was smiling but he knew there had to be something wrong. His paw would have never gone to buy a boat, he would have built it himself using his skills to craft a boat good as the one sitting in the river. He would ask his paw, but not right now, he was going to enjoy some good food and the thought of having a better boat to work with.

All through supper Sam talked about Willie jumping out of the tree and killing that boar then how he out smarted the gator. It was not a bad day for a young man of twelve but Willie didn't see it that way. He just felt that he did what he had to and it wasn't a big deal. To tell the truth, after Willie had jumped on that hog and killed him, he just sat there. The truth be known, his legs were so weak he couldn't stand up but he didn't want Sam to know. It had scared the daylights out of him.

After supper they went to the shed and skinned the animals out. They hung the skins up and carried the remains to the river throwing them in for the gators to eat. Leaving them in the shed would draw the coyote in close and that was not a good thing to do. It was late so Sam stayed the night. They got cleaned up and sat on the porch watching the moon come up. It was so large that it was almost like the dawn, lighting up the river and the swamp. The night was warm but not too hot and a breeze was blowing. Willie sat looking up at the stars and thanked the good lord for the day. He was worried about his paw but wouldn't let on that he knew something was wrong. Tomorrow would be a new day and he would face it and be glad that he had his family to share it with. He stood up and looked at Sam. He started to tell him he was going to bed but he noticed Sam lying on his blanket, sound asleep. It had been a long day and the only things making any noise were the crickets and frogs. The swamp was its own creature, a living soul to itself and Willie loved living here. He closed the door as he entered the cabin muffling the sounds of the swamp and blew out the lamp.

Chapter 4

HARD LESSONS

A month before his fifteenth birthday Willie Cane already had a reputation. He now stood six foot two inches, had cold black hair and a muscular build. He had become tough and fearless. He knew the swamp and from things that had happened and the stories told about him, he was known throughout the south. The incident in Mobile had spread and now the swamp was making him famous. He passed by Two Toes regularly just to keep an eye on him. He had a respect for the big gator and would often take the animal remains to the part of Rice Creek where the big fellow stayed. The boat that his paw had bought was big and carried a lot of weight. They would use it now to make trips to Mobile.

Walter grew sicker and couldn't go too far without having to stop and rest. Even being sick, he would not give up. He continued to trap and work with Willie.

One morning in early September, Walter woke Willie and told him they needed to get moving. The traps up near Fort Mims had been sitting for three days and they needed to be checked. Willie got dressed quickly and Janine had poured up some coffee and made them a good breakfast of eggs and bacon. After getting a sack of deer jerky and biscuits they shoved off towards Fort Mims. It was a damp morning, the fog was so thick you could write in it. You could sit still and get soaking wet at the same time. They stayed near the bank and worked their way to Rice Creek then went up the Tensaw toward the fort. Two Toes was at the edge of the bank and Willie threw a dead chicken towards him. The old gator eased over to the chicken and grabbed it then slid beneath the surface.

It was quiet except for the sound of the oars in the water. Limbs hanging over the banks edge were dripping from the mist that was heavy as rain. Walter was paddling when he eased his oar to his lap and began talking to Willie.

"Son," Walter said, "you know I am proud of you and I have tried to teach you all I can in a short time. Thing is, you have probably taught me more than I have taught you." Willie looked at his paw as if he was trying to understand what he was saying. Walter continued, "If something should happen to me I need you to take care of your maw, can you promise me that son?"

"Paw," Willie said, "what are you talking about? You have had a rough time with the sickness and all but you are strong, you are going to be here a long time yet."

"Just promise me son," Walter said, "I need to know that you will tend to your maw if something happens. Come on now, I need to hear you promise."

Willie looked down at the bottom of the boat then back at his paw. "You know I will Paw but let's not talk about that," Willie said. "You are fine Paw, I will take up more of the load so you can rest more. You and maw have taught me a lot so you two need to start taking it easy and let me take care of ya'll."

Walter smiled and said, "That is a mighty fine comfort son, but you have to realize you'll be finding you a woman in a couple of years and you will need to take care of her."

"Well," Willie said, "that ain't happened yet. I don't speck it will anytime soon so until that day comes, I will take care of ya'll."

"Just remember Willie," Walter said, "look for a woman that makes you happy and understands what you do. Make sure she is willing to be there for you no matter what happens, a woman like your maw. Make sure she understands the swamp life and is able to handle the harsh nature of it. You find yourself a woman like that and you will have a good life."

"It will be hard finding a good woman like Maw," Willie said.

Walter looked at Willie and said, "Yep, it sure will but there is one out there and you will meet her someday. When you do, you will know straight off and then you go after her with all the charm you can muster. See Willie, this swamp is mean and there are a lot of things that make it scary. To overcome that you need somebody to share your time with, if not, you will end up alone and lonely."

"I will remember that Paw," Willie said. All the time he was thinking that his paw was hiding something from him. The day had a strange and eerie feeling to it. Going up to that fort wasn't helping anything. It was the only place near the swamp that Willie didn't like to go and everyone knew it.

The rest of the trip was quiet and took about an hour to reach against the current. The trip took a toll on Walter, and Willie could see his paw struggling to catch his breath. Willie told him to sit there and rest for a spell while he went to check the traps. As Willie was fixing to head out, Walter stood and told him he would check the four traps nearest the boat and that he would sit and wait on Willie to return. Willie nodded and then headed out.

It was just past midday when Willie started back to the boat. The traps had not done that well. He had two foxes and a coon to show for twenty traps. As he started down the path he caught a glimpse of a lady standing by a tree. It scared him a little and he dropped the raccoon to the ground. She was very pretty with a white blouse and a long skirt. She had a wide band around her head with long black hair down below her shoulders. She just stood there but she didn't say anything, just smiled at Willie. He looked at her and he tipped his hat. He leaned over to pick up the raccoon and when he looked back up she was gone. Now he was scared but he wasn't going to tell anyone he saw her. They would think he was crazy.

The fog was still thick but it seemed that the sun was beginning to burn it off and Willie could see the thin outline of the sun coming through. Willie neared the river and found the boat. He placed the catch in the boat and turned looking for his paw. He was not there and it didn't look like he had been back to the boat since early that morning.

Willie began to call out to his paw but there was no answer. The wind started blowing a little and the fog began to move out. Willie walked out in the direction of the traps his paw was going to check. He was calling but the only thing that he could hear was the wind blowing. It had blown the fog away and some dark clouds had begun to build to the south. A storm was coming and the temperature was beginning to fall. Willie needed to find his paw and fast. They may have to set up a shelter and stay put until the storm passed. The wind picked up heavily and seemed to come and go and then the rain began to fall. It was strange the way the wind would come then ease up and the rain would go sideways then slack up. The clouds were moving fast and Willie could feel pressure in his ears. This was not like any storm Willie had seen before. He felt he had to hurry and find his paw and get home if they could.

As Willie neared the third trap, he saw his paw. He was laying by a tree, his head turned towards the east. He held his sack in his hands on his chest. It was as if he had laid there to rest. Willie felt the wind and rain pelting him but he just sat down by his paw and covered him with his coat. He then knew why his paw had made him promise to take care of his maw. He sat there for a while and just cried.

Looking to the heavens with the wind howling and the rain stinging his face, Willie asked God why it had to be this way, why his paw had to die and leave him here in this horrible place. Remembering his paw's words and the promise he made, he picked his paw up and placed him over his shoulder. He struggled but made it back to the boat which had taken on a good bit of water, Willie knew he would not make it back home in the storm so he drug the boat out of the river and turned it over on top of him and his paw. He covered his paw with a tarp and took some rope and tied the boat down so that the wind wouldn't blow it away. He then climbed under it and waited for the wind to stop. Several hours passed and the storm kept blowing and rain falling. All of a sudden it was gone and Willie climbed out from under the boat. The sun was shining and the wind had all but stopped. He could still see clouds coming at them from the south but everything looked to be calm. He was fixing to take the ropes off when he felt the wind shift. It had started from the southwest but now it seemed to be coming out northeast and was beginning to blow hard again. The rain started again so Willie climbed back under the boat and waited.

Willie looked at the canvas covering his paw and wept. He remembered all the things they had done and how his paw had taught him how to work and survive in the swamp. He knew things would now be his responsibility and he would keep his promise to his paw. After a few more hours the winds and rain subsided and the darkness began to fall over the swamp. It was too late to try and get back down the river in the dark. The skies had cleared and the stars just started to break the evening sky. The storm had blown large trees down all around Willie but thankfully none had fell on the boat. It was the worst storm Willie had ever been in and it lasted a long time.

Willie left the boat and went towards the old fort to find some dry wood. He found some that was shielded by the wall and gathered it taking it back to the river. He also feared that the river may rise so he pulled the boat back up the hill just in case. After getting a fire started he secured his paw in the canvas and then pitched a tent with another piece of canvas from the boat. After drying out, he ate some of the deer jerky and biscuits that were left. He sit in silence for a long time listening to the cicada's. They were so loud that there noises drowned out every other sound in the swamp. In a way it was calming to Willie because he still didn't like Fort Mims. He didn't want to hear the strange noises he had been told about that came from the fort at night. In thinking about it, he now knew that his paw may be one that left his soul here to join those that had died in this same place. The only thing he could think about was getting his paw home and wondering how his maw was going to deal with it. He had to be strong, a hard thing to ask a young man to do, but he had to, he had promised, and a Cane never went back on a promise. The night dragged and seemed to last forever but Willie finally fell off to sleep.

Willie woke to a few birds chirping and the sound of the river. It had risen over night and was inching up over the banks. He up righted the boat and got it to the edge. After getting his paw in the boat and loading it, he shoved off. The current was strong and pushed the boat down the river. All Willie had to do was keep it straight. He knew his maw probably hadn't slept, worrying about them. He didn't know what to say to her when he got there. How was he going to look at her and tell her that her husband and his paw was dead? It just didn't seem right for a fourteen year old to have to shoulder such a big responsibility. As the boat moved with the current, Willie cried, he knew he didn't want to cry in front of his maw, it was going to be bad enough like things were. As the boat drifted out of Rice Creek into the Tensaw, Willie looked for Two Toes but the gator was nowhere to be seen. It was a good thing because Willie had no desire to be fooling with the gator today. The storm had put the river over its bank and into the swamp causing the animals to head for high ground.

As he steered the boat around the bend of the river he could see his maw and Sam standing at the edge of the swollen river. Sam started waving but then his hand went down. Janine was standing there with her hands by her side and then slowly took her apron up in her hands, lifting it to her face. Before Willie reached the bank, Janine knew something bad was wrong. Sam wrapped his arm around her trying to console her but she knew. Willie guided the boat to shore and Sam helped him pull it up on the bank. Willie turned to look at his maw and she stood looking at him. He walked up to her and she grabbed him holding him so tight that he could hardly breathe.

"I am sorry maw," Willie said, "I found him laying by a tree, but I couldn't get us home because of the storm."

Janine was sobbing but said "It ain't your fault son. I knew it was coming, just didn't know when."

Janine was trying to be strong for Willie but it was hard. Walter had been the only man she had ever loved, he and Willie were all she lived for on this earth. It hurt so bad but she knew that she needed to be here for Willie. He was still young but had more than proven himself as able to do what was needed to help take care of them.

"Sam," Janine said, "would you mind helping Willie get his paw into the cabin then go fetch Dr. Bettner. We need to get Walter ready for burying."

"Yes ma'am," Sam said, "and I am sure sorry Mrs. Janine."

"Thank you Sam," Janine replied.

Willie and Sam took the body to the cabin and Sam left for Stockton. Within a couple of hours Sam returned with Dr. Bettner and Mrs. Hooper. Dr. Bettner handled just about everything in town and wasn't really a doctor. He was the undertaker and the veterinarian. In working on animals, everybody just called him "doc," so he took up the torch and would try and help tend to folks when they got sick. He wasn't that bad either. He kind of worked on people like he did animals and for some strange reason his methods helped out many a folk in the area. He brought his buckboard and they loaded Walters body up on it. He would take him back to town and build a coffin for him.

Mrs. Hooper came to help Janine and Willie. There was no reason for them to be alone right now. Mrs. Hooper was hurting as bad as they were. She would stay and help them for a few days till the funeral and make sure they were back on their feet. It was the neighborly thing to do because in these parts, neighbors were all you had and the Canes were just like family to her.

Janine sat in the rocking chair in her bedroom. She rocked back and forth looking out the window at the river. It was a place she had sat time and again waiting on Walter to return from his trapping and hunting. Now she would devote her time into Willie making sure he knew what was needed to survive and how much his paw loved him. It would be tough but she knew Walter would be watching them. Willie was young yet he had become a man quickly. Maybe too quickly because he hadn't had the chance to be a kid. It was all part of growing up in a place where kids had to grow up quick. Willie would be fine and she would go on, no matter how hard it might be.

Sam had stayed close to Willie, knowing Willie was hurting and had a heavy heart. There wasn't much Sam could do but be there to help Willie if he needed it. Willie had been quiet since he had gotten back, not saying much about what happened. The storm had blown some trees down so Willie and Sam started cutting them up and stacking them for stove and firewood. The day seemed to drag, but Mrs. Hooper fixed a good super and the two young men had worked up an appetite. They both ate and got cleaned up for bed. Tomorrow was going to be a long day.

As the sun rose, Willie and Sam hooked Flame up to the wagon. They dressed as nicely as they could and loaded up in the wagon to head to town. The ride was bumpy and a little rough with the trees down but they worked their way to Doc Bettner's office. At around ten in the morning Walters wooden casket was loaded on the buckboard. Other families had gathered and would follow the group about two miles to a place called Jug Lake. It was not the city cemetery but it was well known for laying the families of the swamp to rest.

Jug Lake was surrounded by the swamp with one old logging road that led into it. It was a beautiful and peaceful place in the swamp. The road ended at the opening of the lake. The lake was lined with cypress trees, heavy with Spanish moss. Just at the end of the road and to the right was an old picket fence, worn from the years of being weather beaten. The old cemetery had several willow trees, called "Weeping Willows", the limbs of the trees hung down until they almost touched the ground. Wild honeysuckle vines hung off of the fence and the flowers gave off an aroma that was pleasant. A grave for Walter had been dug early that morning by some men from town. Willie, Sam and some other men took the pine coffin and walked over to the grave edge, gently sitting it on the ground.

Charlie Stagner, the preacher from the Baptist church, said a few words and let the visitors pay their last respects. The casket was then lifted onto three ropes hanging over the grave and gently let down into the hole. Janine held Willie and wept as they each grabbed a hand full of dirt and threw it onto the casket. Walter was laid with his head facing to the east so that he could see his maker first. After the casket was lowered the people walked back to their wagons for the trip back to town. Claire had food brought in and they would all meet back there to eat and pay their condolences to the Cane family. Willie was walking beside his mother and Sam was just behind them.

"Sam," Willie asked, "see that willow over there to itself, the one closest to the lake? The one just past my paws grave."

"Yeah," replied Sam, "What about it?"

Willie continued, "If anything ever happens to me, that is where I want ya'll to put me. It is the nicest place here and I can be close to paw and maw when the time comes."

"If I am around, then I will make sure of it," replied Sam.

Back at Mrs. Hooper's place food was stacked up. There were a lot of folks that came by and wished Janine and Willie well, offering their help if needed. Willie watched the people and his eye caught on one pretty young girl. She watched Willie, smiling at him every once in a while. He was going to talk with her but was caught up with other folks and the next thing he knew, she was gone. He had seen her at church but was too shy to say anything to her. Willie would have liked to have known who she was but it was a small town and he was sure he would run into her again. Besides she looked to be older than him and he wasn't really looking for any girlfriends.

The afternoon came and everyone headed home. Mrs. Hooper was going back to help Janine a few days but Janine assured her that she and Willie would be fine. It took some talking but Mrs. Hooper finally gave in and promised to come check on them in a couple of days. The trip back home was quiet and not much was said. Willie could see that his maw was thinking of paw but he didn't know what he could do to help. At the cabin he helped his maw down and unhitched Flame. He fed the animals and went inside. Janine was sitting in the rocker looking out the window.

"You hungry?" Janie asked Willie.

Even though he was a little hungry, he didn't want to bother her.

"They sent a lot of food with us maw," Willie explained. "I got plenty to choose from, you just get some rest, I will tend to it myself."

"Okay son," Janine said. "I think I am going to bed." She got up and went to the bedroom closing the door behind her.

Willie fixed himself some food and ate. As he sat by the fire he could hear his maw crying and it made him sad. He had made a promise to his paw and he would hold to it. He was going to make sure to take care of her in every way he could, but mending her heart was something he just didn't know how to handle. It was going to be tough but they would make it. He listened to the crackle of the fire. Tomorrow would start a new day and he would have to be the man of this family now. It would be hard, but he made a promise.

Chapter 5

A BEAR SIGHTING

It had been two years since the death of his paw and at sixteen, Willie had more experience in the woods and swamp than any man three times his age. He had earned enough money to pay for what was needed and put some back for safe keeping, getting whatever his maw needed. He caught fish and killed animals for food. He had learned to plant a garden and his maw worked it while he trapped and fished. Things had changed a lot since his paw died. Willie had bought a motor that would push the boat better than he could paddle it. He had purchased a motor that was placed on the back of the boat, three horsepower, well worth the money he paid for it. Old Two Toes would come swimming out at Willie when he heard him coming and the two had learned a respect for each other. Willie was still throwing parts of skinned animals to the gator and it was now more of a game to see how far the gator would follow Willie down the river.

The morning was cool on this particular day, only a couple weeks before Easter. Spring was on the doorstep and everything was blooming. On this day Willie was going up towards Dennis Creek to scout out some new places to set some traps. He left early, telling his maw he would be back well before dark. As he was passing Lower Bryant he noticed Sam getting into his boat. He pulled up and spoke with him. Sam was going to check his steel. He made moonshine and to keep people from finding it, he had moved the steel to an island off of Rice Creek. They spoke for a minute and Willie told Sam where he was going. That was always a good thing to do in case you got into trouble. They made plans to go fishing in the afternoon and went on their way.

Willie made it to Dennis Creek and set out looking for good places to set traps. This was not an area he had trapped much but the sign of animals looked promising. He took several traps and began to set them just off of the creek. After about an hour Willie started back to the boat when he heard a rustle in the bushes. He stood still for a moment and out of the brush came two bear cubs. They were playing with each other and both saw Willie about the same time. One of them was curious and began to walk towards Willie while the other just sat there looking. They were Black Bears and Willie knew that their maw was somewhere close by. He didn't want to make any sudden moves to scare the cubs because they may start bellowing and if that happened he would have a mad mama bear after him. The curious cub got within three feet of Willie and stood up on his hind feet. He let out a high pitched growl and Willie started speaking to him.

"Go away fellow," Willie said. "Get on back to your maw, now scat." Willie lifter his hat from his head and waved it at the cub, hoping to make him run off. The second cub bear started doing exactly what Willie did not want. Willie froze and didn't make any moves. The cub nearest him sat back down and ran back to the other cub. Willie breathed a sigh of relief but his sigh was a little too late.

Willie was caught by the big bear's paw across the left shoulder. She had come from his left and he never saw her. The blow from the claws ripped Willie's shoulder open and sent him tumbling to the ground. The bear was on top of him, biting his arms and legs. Willie tried his best to cover his head. He knew if she got him around the neck or head she could crush his skull. He laid face down and that bear hit him two more times, ripping his shirt off and leaving gashes across his back. The bear then picked him up like a rag and slung him across the ground striking him in the chest with those claws. Willie managed to roll over again as she came at him. He rolled up in a ball and lay still. The big bear bumped him several times and Willie lay as if he was dead.

After what seemed an eternity, the bear walked over to the cubs. She never took her eyes off of Willie and even ran at him twice, growling and roaring as if she was trying to get him to move. Willie opened his eyes but blood kept blocking his view. The cuts coming from the wounds on his head made it so that he couldn't see her. The cubs ran towards the woods behind him and disappeared into the brush. The bear walked over to Willie and then walked around behind him. He could feel her breathing on his neck as if she was hoping he would move. After several minutes she walked around him and finally went in the same direction at the cubs. Willie still did not move. He didn't know if she had left the area or not and if she came after him again, he would be finished.

After about an hour Willie knew he needed to get to the boat or he would die. He had lost a lot of blood and had passed out a few times. He didn't know what time of the day it was but he knew he needed to move. He could feel the blood coming out of the cuts but managed to crawl to the edge of the creek, He started covering the gashes with mud to help stop the bleeding and managed to cover the ones he could reach. Willie laid in the mud on his back and squirmed back and forth to get the mud into the cuts. He then tried to get to his feet but was too weak and ended up sitting by a water oak. It had now been several hours since the bear attacked him and the sun was starting to go down in the west. It was not a good situation to be in because of the coyotes and the hogs. Being as weak as he was, there was no way Willie would be able to fight them off. He made it to his feet and started walking towards the boat. After only a hundred yards or so Willie fell face down to the ground and passed out.

"Willie," Sam said, as he shook him. "Wake up Willie, come on my friend, wake up." Willie opened his eyes and saw Sam standing over him.

"Sam," Willie said, "bear got me, she got me good."

"You just hang on, I am going to get you home, you just hang on," Sam said. "My Lord Willie, you are sure messed up. Goanna take some doing to get you fixed back up, what did you do, piss that bear off?"

Willie was in pain but managed to smile a little and said, "Was playing with her children, don't think she liked me doing that."

"I 'speck you're right about that," Sam said. "Now I am going to get you back to the boat, you don't move around too much, don't want to open those wounds again. The mud seems to be holding 'em closed pretty good." Sam was still talking when Willie passed out again. The next thing Willie remembered was pulling up to the landing and Sam yelling for some help. Three men came and helped get Willie out of the boat to Doctor Bettner's place. Willie kept falling in and out of consciousness. Mrs. Hooper came in and started helping Doc work on Willie.

"Go fetch Mrs. Cane." Claire said to Sam. "She will need be here in case this goes bad."

Sam took out the door and borrowed a horse to get to Mrs. Cane as fast as he could. It took a little over an hour but Sam brought Mrs. Cane back. Doc Bettner and Mrs. Hooper had worked hard to get Willie's wounds tended to and had patched him up. He had lost a lot of blood and was not awake when Mrs. Cane entered the room. Doc Bettner had stitched Willie up the best that he could, but the cuts were deep and if Willie made it, he would need some time to heal. Mrs. Cane walked over and kissed Willie's forehead and started to cry. Mrs. Hooper took her and led her away.

"He is a fighter, Janine," Claire said. "He is stronger than anybody else I know, he will be okay, the good Lord willing." She hugged Janine and repeated, "He is a fighter." In her thoughts Mrs. Hooper was asking herself, if he lost too much blood. Only time would tell. She hoped, and she would pray because it was out of their hands. God would have to do the rest.

Willie came to the next morning and was hurting something bad. He remembered the bear and what he had done to protect himself but the rest was fuzzy to him. He was weak and when he tried to get up he didn't have the strength. He was going to call out to someone because he didn't know where he was, nothing looked familiar. Just then the door opened and in walked Dr. Bettner.

"Well now, welcome back Willie," Doc Bettner said. "We wasn't sure you would make it last night. That old bear got you good and you lost some blood."

"Who found me?" asked Willie.

"Sam," Doc replied, "said you talked to him".

"Don't remember," Willie said. "Most I remember is crawling to the creek and that was about it."

"Well son," Doc Bettner said, "your instinct took over and you got the bleeding to stop by putting mud in your wounds. Took Mrs. Hooper and me some doing to get them cleaned up but I got them stitched."

"Where is my maw?" Willie asked.

"She is at Mrs. Hooper's." Doc. Bettner said, "She stayed a long time with you but we made her go get some rest. She'll be along directly. You hungry?"

Willie nodded and said, "Think I could eat a bear."

Doc Bettner smiled and said "Well let's just start with some soup and then you can work up to the bear."

"Sounds good Doc," Willie said. "Thanks for working on me!"

"No problem son," Doc responded, "now you just lay there and rest while I see if I can find you some grub."

After about thirty minutes Doc Bettner returned with some homemade vegetable soup and eggs with a couple of fried chicken legs. Willie ate everything and was already feeling better. He was enjoying the soup when his mom walked in and began smiling as soon as she walked through the door.

"Willie," Janine said, "I knew my prayers would be answered. I knew the good lord wouldn't take you away from me."

"No maw," said Willie, "He figured I had better keep my promise to paw. I am sure fired sore but I will get back to those traps tomorrow."

"Hold on, Willie," Doc Bettner interrupted, "you are going to need a few good days of rest before you go back out in that swamp. You mess around and open up them cuts and you may not be so lucky next go round."

"But I can't let my traps go up in Dennis, they are my best and I had some good sign up there," Willie said.

Janine spoke using one of the strongest voices Willie had ever heard come from her. "Willie Cane, you will do as the doctor has told you. We will get Sam to go check those traps for you."

Willie was only sixteen, but there was one thing he knew and that was to respect his elders, his maw and paw. He had never sassed or had an angry word with them, and he wasn't going to start now.

"Yes ma'am," Willie said.

"We have what we need for right now, you just get well, that is all I want," Janine said.

After a visit, Janine told Willie she was going to return to the cabin and take care of the animals. He was staying with Doc Bettner one more night and Sam would bring him home in the morning.

Willie laid around most all day, sleeping and moving his body around. It seemed that he could not move any way that didn't hurt. He dosed off and then could hear a soft voice speaking to him. He opened his eyes and gasped.

A young girl was standing there looking at him. He finally woke up enough to remember where he was but the girl was still there.

"Who are you?" Willie asked.

"My name is Molly," she said, "You the fellow that the bear got a hold of?"

"Yeah," Willie replied, "you just come here to see if I was dead or not?"

"No," Molly said, "I am glad you are okay. I came to see Doc Bettner and get some medicine for some of my sick brothers and sisters."

"My name is Willie," he said.

"I know who you are," Molly said. "I have heard a lot about you."

Willie was bothered by the young girl, and wanted to go back to sleep.

"Well I am glad to meet you Molly," Willie said.

She nodded and half smiled. About the time Willie was going to speak again, the door opened and Doc Bettner walked in. Molly immediately told him that she had come to pick up some medicine and Doc Bettner gave her what she needed. She then started out the door but stopped as she opened it.

"You take care of yourself Mr. Cane," Molly said.

Before Willie could say anything else to her she was gone.

Doc. Bettner brought Willie some more food and he ate it as if his stomach was touching his backbone. The sun had gone down and the sounds of the small town could be heard. Stockton had four saloons, a general store, a church, and post office with maybe ten families nearby. The saloons were used mostly by the shippers and farm hands. Two of them had rooms upstairs. Never too much excitement but enough noise to keep you awake. Willie lay there thinking about the traps. He only hoped that he would get back to them real soon. As he lay there he listened until the sounds of the saloons stopped and the owls took over the night noises. That was more like the sound he wanted to hear. The crickets were singing, and with the calmness of the night Willie fell off to sleep.

Sam was there early and brought the buckboard for Willie to lay in but he wouldn't. He sat down beside Sam in the seat and they headed to the cabin. Every bump that they hit made Willie hurt to the point that by the time they made it to the cabin, Willie felt worn out. With help he got inside and his maw put him in the bed making him rest and lay still.

Even though it was only a week or so, it seemed like a year that Willie had to stay at the cabin. Sam had followed his directions and picked up the traps in Dennis Creek and done well with them. The only thing that worried Willie was that supplies needed to be bought, he wasn't sure how much money he had saved up for him and his maw. He needed to get back to hunting and fishing and he was more than ready to.

Willie told his maw he was ready to get back to work and she advised him to take it easy. If he was going anywhere, he needed to go with Sam just in case he had problems. He agreed and waited for Sam to come by, which was at least every other day.

Sam made his rounds and was glad to see Willie up and about. Willie was grateful to Sam for saving his life and helping in this hard time. They discussed setting the traps back at Dennis Creek because of the good luck they had. They loaded the boat and headed towards the creek when Sam told Willie he had to make a stop on Hastie Lake. He had to drop some moonshine off to Mr. Brewer, a hermit that lived pretty much alone. Mr. Brewer was like Willie with hunting and fishing, but a lot older. He was a stout middle aged man with not a hair on his head. He had battled these swamps for years and had scars to prove it, but the one thing he liked a little more than hunting and trapping was a good jolt of white lightning every now and then. He was a friendly sort of fellow that tinkered with boats and swapped things to make ends meet. If you needed something built or fixed, just call on him, he would fix you up. You always needed to be careful of what you asked for because you never knew where it may have come from. This wasn't to say that Mr. Brewer was dishonest, just that he had ways of getting stuff.

After dropping off the shine, Willie and Sam headed to Dennis and began setting traps. Willie would rest every now and then because he still didn't have all of his strength back. As they were setting the last few traps they walked into a clearing. Willie froze in his tracks.

Sam was behind Willie and came up beside him with Willie holding his hand out to stop Sam. In the clearing, the same one that Sam had been attacked by the bear was a lone cub. There was a stench in the air of a rotting corpse and the cub was sitting and looking at Willie. He was not moving but watching Willie and acted as if he was injured. The corpse was in the edge of the woods and was huge. Willie and Sam started moving towards the cub very slowly.

As they neared Willie could see that the corpse was the big mama bear that had attacked him. She had apparently been dead several days and from the looks of it, had been shot. The other cub was nowhere to be seen.

"Sam," Willie said, "that was the bear that might near killed me and that is her cub. I don't see the other one."

"Well sir," Sam said, "looks as if someone got her before she got them, it's a shame for that cub though."

"Yeah," Willie said. "that cub want last long out here by himself, hogs or coyote will get him."

Willie took a biscuit out of his bag and poured some honey on it. He walked up to the cub and eased it down for the cub to smell. The cub took it from Willie and ate it. Willie stood looking at the cub and fixed another biscuit for him. He turned and walked back to Sam and when he stopped he felt a tug on his leg. The cub had followed him and was pulling on the tote sack that Willie had around his neck. Willie bent down and rubbed on the cub that responded by rolling over on his back and gently pawing at Willie's hand. The cub was still hungry so Sam fed him some more out of his sack.

"Well," Willie said, "can't just leave him here for the other animals to get, might as well take him home with us."

Sam just smiled and said, "Funniest thing I ever saw. Willie, you are one strange person but I have to hand it to you, you know your animals and this cub has taken a liking to you. Can't wait to see what your maw is going to say!"

"Yeah, me either," Willie exclaimed. "She may have a word or two to say, so let's get to moving and head on home so I can get it over with."

They got to the boat with the cub following in Willie's

tracks. When the cub was picked up, he squirmed a little at first but quickly settled down after exploring everything in the boat. He then curled up on a burlap bag and went to sleep.

On their way back, Sam had Willie pull off of the river and up into Briar Lake. There on an island, Sam tended to his steel and stoked a fire for making his moonshine. Willie watched Sam mix the ingredients and watched how the liquid was made. Sam explained the details of how to set up the still and try to keep it where revenuers couldn't find it. Sam said he worked it mostly at night when he knew the law wouldn't be around. He got the fixings for it from an old Indian from the reservation. The Indian had a connection with the government and got the supplies from an agent in exchange for some of the shine. After watching and getting the bear cub out of the sugar, they finished up and then headed on back to the cabin.

Janine met them and looked at the cub sitting by Willie. Willie explained about what they had found and told his maw he just wanted to make sure the little fellow had a chance.

"Willie," Janine said, "you are just like you paw. The both of you have a way with animals and a heart big as anything when it comes to taking care of em. You can keep him but you have to tend him and make sure he stays out of trouble. When he gets big enough, he is to be let go to the woods where he belongs."

"Yes ma'am," Willie replied.

Sam unloaded the boat while Willie went to get the cub some more food. They sat on the porch as the evening sun was going down and the cub played in the yard. After

dark, Willie led the cub to the storage shed and placed some burlap sacks on the ground in an empty stall back in the corner. After getting Flame in and closing up the chickens, Willie decided to check on the cub one last time and found him curled up and asleep for the night.

Willie's thoughts were on the cub's mama and how strange it was that she had almost killed him to save those cubs and now he was tending to one of them. Life was strange by itself, but this was another life lesson for him. It had been a long day and Willie was not back to himself as for his strength. Setting those traps, learning how to make shine, and dealing with the bear cub had made his day eventful and had tired him out so he decided to turn in.

Chapter 6

HAUNTING PAST

That cub grew quickly and Willie's wounds healed, leaving scars that were hidden by his clothes. Everywhere you saw Willie, the bear was nearby, rummaging through brush hunting something to eat. The bear had gotten attached to the taste of sweet potatoes and Willie noticed every time he would yell "yam's," that bear would come, no matter where he was, so that is what he named the bear, "Yam."

The bear grew large and roamed the land around the cabin at free will. He was never pinned up and never caused a problem. In the winter he would find a place to hibernate and Willie would wait until Yam would show back up in the spring. It was like home coming every year as the bear would play with Willie. They would roll around in the yard and chase each other; then they would climb in the boat and go fishing and run the traps. Yam liked fishing and would end up usually eating half the fish Willie caught if he wasn't watched. As for Two Toes, the respect continued as the gator came to Willie's boat and waited for handouts. The understanding and respect that Willie had for Two Toes was

a story unto itself and Willie's name was well know because of the gator and the bear.

That wasn't all that Willie had become popular for, as he had refined his skills in making moonshine. He tended it and got better at making it to the point that he had people from Montgomery and Mobile making trips to his place to get it. Revenuers knew it too, but they had heard tales of Willie and to tell the truth, were just too darn afraid to go after him. They didn't like the bear and sure didn't want to be a meal for an alligator. Either way, they just didn't mess with him.

It was February, and Willie had to take a load of shine down to Mobile. He was now twenty-one and was a large framed man. He stood six foot three and weighed around two hundred thirty pounds. He was strong and rugged looking, as the weather had worked on him, but still a handsome man. His hair was curly and black and had eyes to match. He had been able to save a sum of money from his moonshine and furs but the biggest thing was his reputation. His name had spread and people had heard of him as far as Huntsville.

With Yam and Two Toes locked down for the winter, it was a good time for him to make the trips down the river. With Two Toes, it didn't matter too much as he was going to stay in his area but, Yam felt like he needed to be right with Willie everywhere he went. It caused a problem because he had gotten too big for the boat, so Willie had to rig up a transom for the raft to place the motor on so Yam could go with him.

Sam met Willie and they loaded the boat with shine to sell in Mobile. It was the Mardi Gras season and people were wanting the moonshine for their parties. Moonshine was something that Willie didn't care much for because he just didn't see himself getting to the point that he didn't know what was going on around him. He would only sample the brew and if it burned on the way down and took your breath for a second then subsided leaving a warm feeling over you, he knew it was ready.

After loading the boat, Willie checked on his maw and told her he would be back in a couple of days. She told him to be careful and make Sam behave himself. Willie and Sam both hugged Janine and the two men headed towards Mobile. The six to seven hour trip had been cut to around two with the motor and the men found a place just outside Mobile to put the moonshine. They hid it and then went on into the city to sell some furs and find buyers for the moonshine. It was a routine that Willie had become accustomed to and knew pretty much who he would sell the moonshine to.

Once they docked, they took the furs to the trading post and sold them. They got a room at the hotel and then after stowing their gear, went to the Silver Slipper to meet with Mr. Mercurio about the moonshine. Mr. Mercurio was a Yankee from New Jersey that had settled here with his family after the war. He opened a saloon and had a gambling room in the back. That was where he sold the moonshine and from what was told, made good money from it. Willie didn't know much about him other than that and, that he loved to talk.

When Sam and Willie arrived at the bar they saw Mr. Mercurio sitting at his table near the end of the bar. They approached him and after a short greetings they discussed the load of moonshine. A price was agreed on and the three sat there talking.

"How long you boys going to be in town?" asked Mr. Mercurio.

Willie answered, "Will be leaving tomorrow evening I guess."

"There is a parade tonight," Mercurio said, "You two need to hang around and see it. There will be a lot of pretty young gals around, you fella's may meet some pretty ones."

Sam was grinning from ear to ear and said, "That sounds good to me."

"We will come by tomorrow around noon and pick up the money, Mr. Mercurio," Willie said. "I don't want to keep it with me at the hotel, that is if that's alright with you."

"That will be fine," Mercurio said. He started to get up from his chair when a rugged looking man in his forties stepped up behind Willie.

"Well, well, well," the stranger said. "I will just be damn if it ain't an old friend of mine," as he touched Willie on the shoulder.

Willie looked up at the man and stood up. They were about the same height but Willie did not know him.

"I am sorry mister," Willie said, "I don't believe I know you."

"Yeah, you know me," said the stranger. "I spent ten years in Huntsville because of you and your paw."

"Mister," Willie said, "I am not looking for trouble with you, but I will promise you that you don't want any with me either."

"Let me introduce myself to you boy," the stranger said. "My name is Paul Grissom, and I want you to remember it."

"Now look here Mr. Grissom, I will have no problems in my establishment," said Mr. Mercurio, as he motioned to the bartender to summons the constables.

"I will be long gone before they get here," said Grissom. "I have a score to settle here and I aim to do it."

"Grissom," Willie said, "it has been a long day and my friend Sam and I are tired and want to get some rest. Now I am fixing to leave this bar and go to my room because to be honest with you, I just don't feel like killing you today."

Willie had already saw the knife in Grissom's hand and knew that he aimed to use it. Willie also knew that he couldn't get to his bowie in time to defend himself so he done exactly what he had been taught by his paw. He reached for his hat with his left hand and when he turned back to his right he swung back to the left as hard as he could. His right fist caught Grissom off guard and square on the chin sending him back over a table behind him. Grissom lost the knife and Willie dove over the table knocking Grissom down as he was trying to get to his feet. The two rolled over a couple of times before Grissom was able to shove Willie off of him with his feet. Grissom was on his feet and as Willie was coming up Grissom caught him just above the left eye busting it open. The blow staggered Willie but as Grissom came in on him Willie swung hard catching Grissom in the ribs and bending him over. Not wasting any time, Willie swung two more times catching Grissom on the chin and in the mouth.

The two men fought, knocking over tables and battering each other. Both were bleeding and after a few minutes Willie got the upper hand and with one final blow, sent Grissom sprawling to the bar room floor. Grissom lay there motionless. The door to the bar opened and Officer Bridges walked in. Willie was leaning over picking up his hat and Sam was helping him keep his balance. Willie was wobbling from the blows he had taken but had once again proven that he was able to take care of himself.

"Well hello, Willie," said Officer Bridges.

"Hey Officer Bridges," Willie responded. "Sorry you had to come, but an old friend of mine had some business he wanted to settle."

"Looks like you handled it well," Bridges said. "Who is it?" he asked.

"Says he is Paul Grissom," said Willie.

"Willie didn't start it Officer Bridges," Mercurio said, "that fella on the floor did."

"I will pay for the damages Mr. Mercurio," said Willie.

"Not to worry son," Mercurio replied, "it was worth the time just watching the fight."

Willie and Sam headed for the door after Officer Bridges told them they could leave. Officer Bridges had helped Grissom to his feet, getting him steady. As Grissom stood, he shoved Bridges with his left arm while grabbing the officer's gun with his right. He then turned toward Willie raising the gun and aiming it him. In hearing the commotion, Willie turned seeing the gun being raised by Grissom. Willie shoved Sam away to the left and threw his bowie knife in one move. The knife went true and caught Grissom in the chest with the gun firing as the knife hit him. The bullet struck a lamp behind Willie and Grissom dropped the gun to the floor. Officer Bridges grabbed the gun as Grissom dropped to both knees looking at Willie.

Grissom struggled to speak saying, "Damn you are good, kid."

"I told you I didn't feel like killing you today," Willie said.

Grissom grinned and fell over.

There was silence for a moment as Sam got up off the floor. Willie walked over and pulled his bowie out of Grissom's chest cleaning the blade on Grissom's shirt. Officer Bridges holstered his gun and checked Grissom for a pulse.

"Well," Bridges said, "I will take care of this but I will need a statement from you two in the morning, Willie."

Willie nodded and said, "Hate it happened this way,"

"It is not your fault Willie," Officer Bridges said, "Grissom was intent on killing you one way or the other. It was self-defense and all I need to do is get it on paper; I will get this taken care of, you two go get some rest or watch the parades or something. I will see you in the morning."

Willie and Sam agreed and walked out of the bar telling Mr. Mercurio they would see him tomorrow as well. As they walked towards the hotel, the parade was passing and they stopped and watched for a while. They then went on to the room.

Willie lay in bed thinking of Grissom and the look on his face. It was bothering him some but he knew Grissom would have killed him. It wasn't like killing an animal, this was a man and Willie had just taken his life.

Sam noticed Willie laying there looking out the window and said, "Willie, you did what you had to. Don't go pondering or fretting on it too much. If you hadn't of killed him, he would have killed you."

Willie nodded and said, "I know, but it still don't make it right for a man to put himself in a situation to get himself killed. I know I did what I had to, but it still don't make it any better."

"You a good man, Willie Cane," Sam said. "Everyone in that bar saw you walk away and that man wasn't going to let it go. It was either him or you, and I am glad it was him, he had it coming."

"Thanks Sam," Willie said, "I appreciate that."

Willie lay there for what seemed like hours but finally fell off to sleep. Sam rolled over and could see the morning light coming through the window. He looked over at Willie's bed but he wasn't in it. Sam got up and dressed then went down to the café. Willie was sitting there looking at the street and how peaceful it looked that early in the morning. After greeting Sam, they ordered breakfast and then headed to the police station.

Officer Bridges had a long night, but was riding up when they got to the building.

"Good Morning," Bridges greeted them. "I hope you fellows slept well."

Sam spoke first, "Well sir, I did but Willie had some things on his mind and I don't believe he got much sleep."

"Well I can make you feel a little better Willie," Bridges said. "Come on in here and I will show you what I found out."

They entered the building which had a large front office area with three desks in it. Behind a half wall were what looked to be about eight prisoner cells. They were empty with the exception of the first one which had two men in it. One was standing by the cell door and the other was asleep on the bunk. It appeared from where the officers sat, they could watch all the cells in case of problems.

Bridges walked to the desk nearest the front door and sat

down. A name plate on the front of the desk had his name "Lieutenant Carlton Bridges." He shuffled through some papers and then pulled out a sheet and handed it to Willie.

"That my friend," said Lieutenant Bridges, "is a wanted poster for one Paul Grissom. He was wanted in Gulfport, Mississippi for Robbery and Murder. There was a five thousand dollar reward for his capture, dead or alive. You have just made yourself a sum of money, Willie."

Willie looked at the poster and said, "I'll be damn, that man really would have killed me."

"Yes," Bridges said, "he sure would have. By the time the chief gets back with the money, you two can write out your statements and be on your way."

They wrote the statements and the chief returned and gave Willie the reward money. They thanked Officer Bridges and then headed over to see Mr. Mercurio. It was still early but he was up and they spoke of where they would meet him with the moonshine. He paid Willie about four hundred for the brew and Sam and Willie headed to the boat and went to the meeting location. After about an hour, Mr. Mercurio and two of his workers met them and took possession of the moonshine.

"We will see you in about a month Mr. Mercurio," Willie said.

"That will be fine," Mercurio said, "you take care of yourself and we will see you then."

The men shoved off and headed back to the swamp. Willie was looking forward to it. The trip back was quiet with the exception of Sam trying to sing. He would bellow out a tune and Willie didn't have the heart to tell him he sounded like cat with its tail caught under a rocking chair, so he just endured the racket. After about an hour, Sam gave out and went to sleep in the bottom of the boat. Willie looked at Sam and thought about how lucky he was to have him as a friend. He was always there if he needed him. That was what friends should do for each other, or at least that was the way he felt.

The trip home took a couple of hours and they finally arrived just after noon. It had been a busy two days but it was sure good being back home. Sam helped Willie unload some supplies and was fixing to leave when Willie stopped him.

"Sam," Willie said, "I want to thank you for helping me and being here for me." He handed Sam a roll of money but Sam was reluctant to take it. "No Sam, you take this, you are my friend and I would give you more if I had it. Not having to face Grissom alone and having you talk with me when I was down meant a lot to me, now take it."

Sam took the money and shook Willie's hand. "Thanks," Sam said, "but you didn't need me to whip that fella, hell you handled him real good and you did what you needed to. You are a good man Willie Cane and a good friend and seems to me good friends don't come along every day. Besides that was one heck of a fight."

"Well let's get a bite to eat and then we will take the rest of the day off and get ready to go trapping tomorrow," Willie said. "I have got to tell maw what happened and I don't want to have to do it by myself if you know what I mean."

"Tell me what?" Janine said as she had walked up behind them.

"Let's get some dinner maw and I will tell you then," Willie said.

She looked at Willie and agreed which gave Willie that

relieved look. Sam didn't say anything, just kept getting supplies out of the boat. After finishing, they sat down at the table and Willie explained to Janine what had happened. She was tough and understood which was surprising. She walked around the table and hugged Willie telling him that God would forgive him and that she knew he could handle himself. She then went to her room and closed the door. Willie could hear her crying and knew he needed to leave her alone for a little while. She was showing her motherly emotions and her room was the place she went to express them in her own way.

Sam let Willie know he would see him in a few days and started off down the road. He looked at the wad of money that Willie had given him and counted twenty-four hundred dollars. A tear came into his eye and he just kept walking, no one had ever been that nice to him. He turned around and waved at Willie and then took off down the road at a fast walk. His family would have good food tonight.

Chapter 7

READING THE STARS

Several years passed and Willie noticed the changes around him. The town, people and even the need for furs had changed. He was still able to sell his moonshine but trapping of furs was no longer a way to make a living. The sawmill was running full blast and most of those that used to work in the cotton fields were now working the timber business, either in the swamps cutting trees or at the mill cutting lumber for shipment. There were these things on roads they called cars and people that could afford them moved around from one place to another very quickly. Willie had heard of them when he bought the motor for the boat but never thought of trying to buy one.

At twenty eight Willie had not settled down with a woman and pretty much stayed to himself with the exception of Sam and Cotton. Cotton was a colored man that lived outside Stockton in a shack. He worked the fields until winter then turned to helping Willie fish and move his moonshine. Cotton was well liked in the community and worked odd jobs for people when they needed things like firewood or gardening. He had no family that anyone knew of and just as Willie, pretty much stayed to himself. He was almost as good as Willie at trapping and fishing, but didn't make moonshine at all. He did what he had to too survive.

Willie's maw had been sick for a while and was down in bed. Willie was going to pick up some medicine from Doc Bettner and walked the six miles into town. The mule Flame had died of age and Willie could see no reason to buy another one. His maw was the one that worked the garden and she had not been well enough to work it for a few years. It was almost as if she had given up and she talked about paw all the time. She was now in bed with a fever and had no energy to get up and move about. Willie remembered his promise to his paw and he was doing everything he could to make his maw comfortable. Sam had plowed a garden with his horse and kept it for her because she always like to have one.

Willie was about a half mile outside town when he noticed a wagon sitting on the side of the road. It looked kind of like a snake oil salesman trailer. On the side of it was the words, "See Your Future," Palm Reading by Tasha. Willie had heard of wagons like this and gypsies that traveled with them. He saw a woman with long black hair and tanned skin walk around the back of the wagon. She looked at him and smiled. Speaking with an accent she greeted Willie.

"Well hello Mr. Cane," the woman said. "I see you are headed to town, is your mother any better?"

Willie was taken by surprise not only by her knowing his name but that he had seen her before. He had never spoken to this woman but he remembered her from Fort Mims in the woods. Yet, she knew his name and about his maw. Another thing that puzzled him was that she wore the same clothes and she looked the same as she did that day.

Willie responded, "She is pretty sick and yeah I am headed to town to pick up some medicine. How did you know all of that?"

"Well," she said with a smile, "I can tell your future but you should not worry, I would have to see your palm for that. A man named Sam came by earlier and told me you may be coming this way and about your mother. I would like to look at your palm though just to see what kind of life you have lived and what your future may be."

Willie, not wanting to offend the woman said, "I really don't believe all that stuff ma'am."

"You don't have to believe it Willie," Tasha said, "just let me take a look at your palm and tell you what I see."

"Ma'am," Willie said, "I really don't have the money for it and I do need to be getting on."

"I will tell you what," Tasha said, "let me read your palm, no more than ten minutes, if you like what I say then you pay me two bits, if not, you don't owe me anything."

Willie thought about it and looked at her. She was really an attractive woman and looked to be in her thirties. She had dark black hair and eyes. She wore a band around her head and a white blouse with a long multi colored skirt that seemed to cover a very nicely shaped body. He looked for anyone else around but saw no one.

"Who are you with ma'am?" Willie asked.

"I am alone Willie," Tasha said. I have some things to do here, but I dare not go into town. They don't like fortune tellers in some of these small towns. I will finish my business here soon and I will be moving on towards Montgomery."

After giving it some thought Willie decided to let her see his palm and went into the wagon with her. He sat down at a table and Tasha stood near him. She took his hand and began to look at the lines.

She started speaking and Willie just sit and listened. "Your past has been one of trials and you have faced each of them without failing a promise that you made. I am sorry but your promise to your father is almost over. Did you make a promise to your father?" Tasha asked.

"Yes," Willie said. Willie knew she was talking about his maw but if she spoke to Sam she would have known that Janine was in very bad shape.

Tasha continued, "I see that you have never had a true love of your own but you will and it will be very soon. You also will befriend a four legged friend that will be by your side until the end." She stopped and looked at Willie, "This is all I can tell you," she said as she quickly let go of his hand and stood up. "There is no charge to you."

Willie watched her and asked her what was wrong? "What did you see?" Willie asked.

"Mr. Cane," Tasha said, "it is sometimes better not to know what our future has in store for us. I feel this very strongly for you, that it is better if you let fate follow its course."

"Tell me what you saw," Willie said, kind of in a demanding manor.

Reluctantly Tasha took his hand again and asked Willie if he was sure he wanted to know? After he assured her he did, she began to read his palm again.

"You will meet a woman and you both will love," Tasha said. "Only her love will be secret and will sadden you.

Things will occur and a bad ending will result from this …" Tasha paused. "I cannot tell you more Mr. Cane that is all. Hold to your heart Mr. Cane and know that you are loved, whether you see it or not."

Willie stood puzzled at what she had said. "Well ma'am," Willie said, "thank you for your time and for the reading. Too bad you have to travel, I would like to have you over for dinner."

"Thank you Willie," she said, "I will come back this way and hold you to it."

Willie laid two dollars on the table and walked out the door. Tasha didn't say anything but followed him to the door. Looking down at him, she said, "Mr. Willie Cane you be careful, you are a good man with a big heart. You are rugged and people both respect and fear you." "This woman that you will meet, you have met before. I wish I could tell you more but I dare not tempt the fate that awaits anyone. We will meet again, this I am most sure of. Take care of yourself."

Willie nodded and headed off down the road pondering the things he had been told. He was unsure if he should believe any of the words that he had heard. As he neared the town he was met by Cotton.

Cotton stopped Willie and said, "You need to get home Willie, things is gone bad for your maw. Doc. Bettner says to use his horse and I already have him saddled for you." Willie had not picked up the medicine and reach in his pocket to hand money to Cotton so that he could pick it up. As he pulled his hand out of his pocket he discovered the two dollars he had left the gypsy. It was as if he had never left her anything.

Willie didn't hesitate, he climbed on the horse heading back to the cabin as fast as he could to see his maw. It was strange, but just outside town where he had met with Tasha there was nothing there. He had not passed anyone coming from town and that was the only one way to get in and out of town. The wagon was gone and there was no sign of any tracks where the wagon had been. Willie looked back at the spot and everything was just gone, as if it had disappeared into the air.

Within a short time, Willie rode up to the cabin and was met by Doc Bettner and Mrs. Hooper.

"You need to hurry son," Doc Bettner said.

Willie walked into the bedroom where his maw lay, her silver hair spread out on the pillow. She turned her head and looked at Willie and held her hand out. Willie took it and sat in the chair by the bed.

"Willie," Janine said, "it is time for me to meet with your paw. I have stayed with you and watched you become a man and you have tendered your promise to your paw and took care of me." Willie started to speak but she stopped him and continued. "I am so tired Willie and last night I saw your paw as clear as if he was here. He was sitting on the bench at the gate waiting on me Willie, and it is time for me to join him."

She pointed to a wooden box on the table and said, "That belongs to you and your children and wife when you find one. It is all your paw and me could keep for you so you use it for what you need. I love you, Willie."

Willie felt his heart sink but he knew his maw had mourned his paws death for a long time.

"I love you maw," Willie said, "don't you worry about me, I will be alright."

Janine smiled at him and he leaned over and kissed her forehead. She was weak but managed to lift her arms and hug him. He sat there holding her hand.

"Look Willie," Janine said, "they are here for me, two angels standing at the window, they are so beautiful."

That was her last words as she closed her eyes with a smile on her face and took her final breath.

Willie walked out of the room after a while to sit on the porch. Cotton and Sam helped Dr. Bettner load his mother on the buckboard for the trip back to town. As he looked out over the river it struck him that he was now alone. He had been taught well by his parents and knew how to cook and clean and take care of himself, but his thoughts were on the loneliness that was to follow. As he sat there, Yam came strolling up to the porch and laid down beside Willie's chair. It was as if Yam knew something was wrong as he took his paw and gently rubbed on Willie's leg. Willie reached down and stroked his head. Yam then half sat up and laid his big head on Willie's leg as if to say, I am here with you my friend. As Willie watched the river, Yam went to sleep and stayed with Willie for hours on the porch.

After everyone had left, Willie stood up and walked down to the river with Yam close behind. Willie watched and as he looked up in the direction of Briar Lake he saw Two Toes laying on a sandbar near the boat. It was unusual for the big gator to get that far from his territory but again it was as if they knew Willie was sad and even though they were wild, they wanted to be near him. As the sun started to set, Two Toes eased back into the water and started back towards Briar Lake and Rice Creek. Yam followed Willie to the barn and watched as he fed the chickens and shut up the barn for the night.

Willie went back to the porch again to sit for a while, listening to the crickets and frogs as they started their night time serenade. Willie had never been much on religion but he looked to the stars and thanked God for giving him parents that loved him and taught him how to survive. Parents that had taught him right from wrong, respect for all men and who took care of him. He also thanked God for making the animals of the swamp his friends and giving him company by them just being there. The darkness of the night swept over the swamp as the owls began screeching and bats flew in the night horizon feasting on any bugs they could catch. It was so quiet that Willie could hear the river as it moved along the banks edge and he felt comfortable. He stood to go into the cabin and Yam waddled to the door behind him. Willie stepped into the door and looked back as Yam circled himself into a ball and laid down in front of the door. Tomorrow would be a long day but it was a time that he was sad and happy about. He was sad because his maw was gone but happy because now she would be with paw and that was what she had waited on the last few years.

Willie got up early and as he opened the door Yam got up from the spot where he had fallen asleep. Yam walked up to Willie and was petted, then he walked off of the porch and into the woods. It was a day that Willie dreaded, not only because he was burying his maw but because people had shunned him a lot since he had killed the man in Mobile. A lot of them had heard the story and most knew that it was self-defense, but others couldn't accept the fact that he had taken a life. Sam had told the story many times and finally, after years, people of the town started talking to Willie again. It was a hard road but he had weathered it pretty good. Most of those people would be at the funeral today and he hoped they would see him as a man that cared and was not the cruel killer that some said he was. Either way, he had to do this for his maw. Cotton showed up with Dr. Bettner's wagon and Willie road to town.

Janine was buried by Walter on Jug Lake. There were a lot of folks there and Willie watched the crowd. He noticed and knew many of the people and they all came and shook his hand wishing him the best and telling him they were sorry for his loss. Willie was polite and thanked them. A young woman stepped up to him and Willie took a deep breath. She was beautiful and he went speechless. She wished him the best and then just walked away. He was fixing to follow her and get her name, but Sam came up to him talking about carrying some moonshine to Jackson. By the time he finished talking the woman was gone and Willie didn't know who she was or anything about her.

Willie was now the last Cane around these parts. He had no kin folks around and he didn't know where any of his other relative's lived or if he even had any. He would carry on and hopefully the woman that the gypsy had told him about was the one at the funeral. She stayed on his mind the rest of the day. Maybe he would not be alone for long, either way, he would go on.

Chapter 8

FORTUNES OF TRUTH

After a year or so Willie sold the cabin and the land. He purchased a houseboat that floated on Tensaw Lake. It took him a while but Willie got the houseboat moved to a spot on Briar Lake that had an acre of land. The land had been cleared so it was easier for him to build a ramp to the houseboat and secure it to large cedar trees on the bank. He built a shed for smoking meat and a shed for drying skin then another shed for Yam to sleep in. The bear followed him through the swamp and seemed to enjoy his new home. Yam still liked to sit with Willie on the porch of the houseboat so Willie had to build an extra sturdy ramp leading to the boat. Yam weighed around five hundred pounds and the houseboat was plenty sturdy enough for him.

Willie also had another old friend close by. Two Toes made his home on Briar Lake and he was always nearby. The old gator was spoiled as he would come up to the houseboat nearly every day waiting for whatever Willie would throw him. Even with both of them there with him, Willie was lonesome. Sam and Cotton would come by and visit, hunting and fishing with him but it was obvious something was missing. The woman Willie had met at the funeral was still a mystery. Willie had not found out who she was and no one had seen her talking to him so he was at a dead end with trying to find her.

Selling the moonshine had become risky but Sam and Willie took chances, always being careful and dealing with only the people they knew. Mr. Mecurio was the best customer and they trusted him. They also had buyers in Jackson and McIntosh which was up the river a ways but still reachable. Their business helped Willie get what he needed. He found that he didn't need much so nothing was pressing. He was putting money back for whenever he may need it..

Early one spring morning Willie went to set some traps near Rice Creek. He had finished setting a couple of traps when he heard a lot of squealing and grunting going on in some pretty heavy palmetto bushes near the bank. He knew it was wild boar and he took his time easing through the swamp to sneak up on them. He had his dad's fifty caliber black powder rife with him and he knew it would easily take a hog down. As he eased into the edge of an opening he saw three hogs at the end of a hollowed out cedar tree that had fallen. The hogs were trying to get through the opening at the end of the tree but couldn't get through the hole. Willie aimed at the smallest of the three hogs and fired. The hog fell in his track and Willie loaded the rifle again.

The other two hogs didn't run off but thirty yards or so then returned to the end of the tree. Willie took aim and dropped the second hog. This time the last hog took off and went through the woods. Willie reloaded just in case the big boar came back. He shot the two smaller hogs because the meat would be tender and easier to work with. As he approached the tree he could hear movement inside the hollow end of the stump. He took the rifle and aimed at the opening. He had no idea what was in the tree but he didn't want to be mauled by a boar coon or mad bobcat. As he watched the opening he saw a head come out and he smiled lowering his rifle. A young dog stuck his head out of the hole and looked up at Willie. The dog looked to be a year old and came out of the hole of the log wagging his tail. Willie spoke to him and the dog came up to him. It appeared that the dog had been around people but was real skinny and needed some food.

Willie patted him on the head and questioned him as to where he came from. It was not uncommon for a dog to get lost in the swamp and never seen again. This dog was lucky that Willie came along. The hogs would have killed him and had him for dinner. Willie gutted the hogs and tied a rope around their legs. They would be too heavy to drag whole. The dog ate his fill of the hogs and as Willie headed back to the boat the dog followed. After getting the hogs loaded, Willie looked back and the dog sat on the bank looking at him. Willie remembered what the gypsy had told him about a four legged friend. He walked over to the dog and reached down, picking the dog up. He set the dog in the boat and shoved off. The dog wasn't very tall and looked to weigh around thirty pounds. He had a long looking body and short legs. He was black with a white stripe on his nose. He also had white under his neck that went between his front legs and along the bottom of his stomach. His two front feet had a mixture of brown and black color to them up to the knees.

"You are a sight for sure," Willie said to the dog. "Since you seemed to bring me good luck with those hogs, I believe I will call you Bait." The dog cocked his head sideways as if he was trying to understand what Willie was saying. Willie continued, "Guess you was what that gypsy lady was talking about being my four legged friend. Now look at me, sitting here talking to you as if you know what I am talking about. Anyway Bait, we will see what you can do and see if you will be good company but first we have a few other friends I have to talk to about you."

Bait had eaten and was sleepy, so he curled up in the boat and went to sleep. Willie headed home with meat to smoke and a new friend.

After arriving back at the houseboat Willie drug the hogs to the cleaning rack and hung them up. He then pulled a barrel out of the shed. He grabbed some wood from the wood pile and placed it into a hole he had dug. The hole was deep on one end and slanted. The wood was set on fire under the barrel, which had been laid into the hole at an angle then filled with water. Cotton came walking up and saw Willie getting ready to clean the hogs.

The water in the barrel began to boil and Willie took the hogs one at a time, rolling them around in the boiling water. He then would pull them out and lay them on a wooden table Cotton took some sharp knives and began scraping the hair off of the hogs. This would clean the skin of the hog and make them better for smoking. After a couple of hours they finished cleaning and cutting up the hogs and placed the hams from them in the smoke house to cure. Willie explained how he got them and Cotton just shook his head.

"I declare Willie," Cotton said, "you is got to be one of

the luckiest peoples I know. Wild hogs is jumpy of folks like it is and you get two and a stray dog to boot, pure ass luck."

Willie smiled and said, "Well I guess what the gypsy lady said come true Cotton." She told me I would be getting a four legged friend and there he is. I named him Bait."

About that time Bait stood up and the hair on the back of his neck bristled as he began to growl. Willie looked and saw Yam coming out of the woods.

"Calm down Bait," Willie said.

Yam eased up to Willie and he rubbed the bears neck. Seeing Willie rub the bear seemed to calm Bait and he started easing towards Yam. The two looked at each other for a while and finally touched each other nose to nose. With that they seemed content and Yam walked off laying down on the porch of the houseboat. Bait laid back down on the ground and continued to watch Cotton and Willie.

"That was easier than I thought," Willie said. "I don't speck it will be that easy with Two Toes. Bait is a good meal for him and I don't think they will be touching noses."

"I believe you are right," Cotton said, "that old gator would think that mutt is fine food or something. Best not trust them to get close or your gypsy ladies tell will be gone."

They finished hanging the meat and Cotton went towards home with some fresh pork for supper. Willie cooked up some chit lens and pork chops with biscuits and gravy and he and Bait had a feast. Willie washed up and went to bed. Bait curled up at the foot of the bed on a deer skin, content to be with Willie. It had been a busy but productive day. Daylight would be here soon enough and Willie would go to hunt some gators for a boot company in Montgomery. His new companion would be with him and he wouldn't be as lonely as he had been, but there was still the woman that he was suppose too meet. He had not forgotten the woman at the funeral.

As the morning sun came over the cedar trees lining Hastie Creek, Willie was busy setting his lines to try and catch some gators. He would need at least four of them measuring at least eight feet each. That would cover the skins he needed for the boot company. Cotton had met him early and they had most of the lines set before good daylight. It was always good to work with someone when catching gators because they were pretty much a hand full. Cotton not only knew how to catch them, he was good at cleaning them and made some fine gator stew and fried gator tail. Willie always paid him for helping and so far they had made a little money from it. They were the only two around that knew how to catch the critters. Willie never hunted them around Briar Lake because of Two Toes. Besides, there weren't any more male gators in that area. It was Two Toes domain and other males would not come anywhere around it.

After setting the lines Cotton and Willie pulled under a low hanging cedar tree and out of the morning sun. The two ate some sausage and biscuits and waited to see if their lines were going to do any good. Cotton seemed to think it would be a good morning for the gators because it was pitch black during the night. Gators would want to eat early so they would be swimming around hunting something to eat on. Willie had used some chicken legs for bait. The legs had been left out a couple of days and were smelling awful bad. Matter of fact, every time the wind would change directions they could smell them, almost bad enough to turn a stomach. That was what the gators liked and they would come fast to grab onto one of those legs as rotten as they were. They smelled so bad, Willies new friend Bait wouldn't even smell them. The best thing was the rotten chicken caught gators and that was all that mattered. Hastie Creek had some fine gators in it and the two men figured to make quick work of catching what they needed and getting home before the sun got too hot.

Willie laid back in the boat and looked up into the cedar tree. About three feet above the boat was a three foot water snake that had curled around the limb for the night and hadn't yet made it back into the water. They were harmless and all, but Willie never said anything about the snake to Cotton because he knew that Cotton was sure fire afraid of snakes, didn't matter what kind or if they were poisonous or not. Willie figured it was best not to scare Cotton so he let it go. The breeze was blowing and would swing the boat around under the edge of the cedar tree. The front of the boat was tied to the very limb that snake was on and it was sure luck that Cotton didn't see it when he was tying up the boat.

After about an hour Willie could hear splashing and knew that one of the lines had a gator. He yelled for Cotton to untie the boat. Now Cotton had fallen off into a deep sleep and he sprang up so fast that he raddled that limb the snake was on. The boat had swung around until that snake was almost over Cotton. When he hit the limb with his shoulder, that snake came falling into the boat and Willie had never seen a grown man cut up like that. Cotton danced around the boat as that snake began to crawl around and after about ten seconds, Cotton bailed out of the boat and into the creek, as if he had some place to be. Lucky they were only in about three foot of water, because as scared as Cotton was, he may have drowned himself. Willie was laughing so hard he had tears coming from his eyes even though he knew how scared Cotton was. Bait had cornered the snake and Willie reached over and grabbed the snake, flinging him out of the boat and back into the creek on the opposite side of Cotton. It wasn't long before Cotton had jumped back in the boat and was panting like he had just finished running from a hog. Willie was still laughing and almost forgot about the gator on the line.

"You scared that snake to death Cotton," Willie said.

"Th, th, that just ain't at all funny Mr. Willie," Cotton said. "You knew that snake was up there and you could've said something. That just wasn't right Mr. Willie." Cotton was stuttering while he was trying to speak.

Willie was still laughing and said, "Cotton, that snake was trying to catch a nap too, you just upset his sleep. Hell, he wasn't going to hurt you."

"Mr. Willie, you know how I is afraid of snakes and I ain't be caring if they can hurts me or not, I sure 'nough don't likes em."

Willie apologized but was still laughing. He tried to hold a straight face, but it was just so hard to do, looking at Cotton dripping wet. After a few minutes of ribbing Cotton sat quiet and began laughing his self.

"Well, at least you got cooled off before we go get that gator," Willie said.

Cotton untied the boat but you can bet he was watching the limbs. They headed to the line that was tight and within a couple of minutes had an eight foot gator in the boat. It took them the better part of the morning but by around ten o'clock they had caught seven gators and pulled up their lines. There were some extra gators to clean and the boot company would buy all of the skins. It was a good morning.

As they started out of Hastie Creek there was a boat coming into the creek that looked to be doing some bream fishing. Hunter Bell was catching up some crappie and bream for a fish fry and a celebration. One of the Bell kids was fixing to leave home for college. Willie didn't know the Bells too well but knew they lived off of Bottle Creek near Miffin Pass. He had met Hunter several times on coon and deer hunts and found him to be a likable fellow. Hunter yelled at them and began talking about the party.

"Hello Mr. Cane," Hunter spoke. "Look, we are having a get together for my sister Nicole. She is turning nineteen and fixing to go off to college up in Tuscaloosa. Would you like to come?"

Willie pondered for a minute then said, "Sure why not, ain't been to a gathering in a while. When is it?"

"It will be this here coming Saturday at around two o'clock," said Hunter. "We would love to have ya and you can bring a couple of jars of that shine if you would like."

"Sure thing," said Willie, "I got some that has been aging and is smooth all the way down to your toes. It is pretty strong though, you won't need too much."

"Sounds good," Hunter said. "We will be looking for you."

They parted ways, Willie and Cotton headed on back to the houseboat to skin the gators. Willie was thinking about the last two days and finally felt like life wasn't so bad. He had a friend in a dog, a laugh at another friend Cotton and now he was invited to a shindig. Things were indeed looking up.

It took them a couple of hours to skin the gators and cut up the meat, but they had plenty. Sam came by and they cooked up a pot of gator stew. Some of the town folks heard about the gators and came to see the catch. It was a lot easier and closer to the town now that Willie had moved his houseboat to Briar Lake. It was only half a mile at most. In all about twelve folks showed up including Doc Bettner, so Cotton fried up some gator tail and they had a shindig of their own. Hunter Bell was heading down the river and saw the goings on and stopped too. It was well past ten at night before folks finally left. There was no moon so it was pitch black and not a good time to be moving on the river. Willie offered Hunter a cot for the night and he agreed to stay, waiting till first light before going back home. He hadn't had too much luck fishing and really felt bad about not catching enough fish for the party. Willie calmed his fears and set two lanterns out at the end of the houseboat. He threw some corn in a croaker sack and flung it into the lake, tying the line off to the house boat. After about thirty minutes he grabbed a couple of cane poles and a can of wigglers.

"Let's go catch you some fish, Hunter," Willie said.

"How?" asked Hunter, "ain't no fish going to bite at night, maybe excepting a catfish."

"Just fish," Willie said. "It is an old trick my paw taught me and we will catch you some fish,"

They caught fish for a couple of hours. They were catching mullet, catfish and bream, which Hunter couldn't believe. After getting what they would need for the party, Hunter fixed up his fish trap and kept them alive until he could get home with them to clean. Hunter thanked Willie for his help in getting what he needed. Cotton was already asleep when Willie and Hunter turned in. When daylight came Hunter left and again thanked Willie for helping him with the catch.

"We'll see you Saturday, Willie," Hunter exclaimed as he shoved his boat off.

"Looking forward to it Hunter," Willie said. "I should be back in time. I have to go to Mobile with these skins and I got some other business there. Will be making the trip alone but it shouldn't be a problem. Will be back on Friday, so I'll see you on Saturday."

Hunter headed on down the lake singing a song to himself and Willie started loading the boat for his trip. It was going to be a good day and hopefully a good weekend, at least it had started that way. As Willie shoved off heading for Mobile, Yam was eating on some left over fish and sweet potatoes. Two Toes was swimming around the house boat looking for leftovers Willie had thrown out for him. Bait was standing on the front of the boat looking out over the river. Cotton decided to go plant a garden for Mrs. Hooper and Sam had other jobs he had to do so this would be a trip Willie would make alone. He did have Bait with him and so far the dog had proven to be a good companion.

The gypsy lady had told him things would change for him. Maybe this was what she meant. He didn't really believe in that stuff but he wasn't going to speak badly about it. Either way, he would take things one day at a time. It was what he had been taught to do and he had no reason to change.

The trip down the river was as usual as any. He stopped

just outside the city and placed the moonshine in a different location than normal. He sure didn't want any lawmen catching him with it. After arriving at the wharf and tying up the boat, Willie went to the trading post with Bait at his heels. The gator skins were shipped and Willie picked up supplies. He stopped in and set up his sells with Mr. Mercurio and then headed back to the wharf. As he finished loading the boat for the trip back up the river he noticed the changes of the wharf. A large warehouse was built and was being used for ships coming in with bananas. Horse and wagon weren't used as much as they use to be. Willie knew there would not be many more trips by river with this thing called the automobile and steam trains carrying goods all over the place. It would be faster to just ship the skins from the train depot in Bay Minette but Willie liked the way he had done it for years.

Willie went to the location he had left the moonshine and waited there for Mr. Mercuro. He sat under an oak and dosed off until Bait began to growl. He stood up waiting to see Mr. Mercurio and his workers just like many times before but something was wrong. He didn't hear the normal jabbering by the Italian which he was known for, never ceasing to talk. Instead Willie didn't hear anything, it was quiet, too quiet, and Bait was looking in the direction of some thick brush. A direction Mr. Mercurio would not be coming from. He decided to call out and see who was there.

Willie called out, "Alright, come on out and show yourself."

About that time three men walked out of the brush. Willie didn't know them but he did recognize one of them. Willie had seen him in the corner at Mr. Mercurio's Bar. It didn't take much figuring to realize that he had overheard the conversation and was here to take the moonshine and Willie's money.

"What can I help you fellow's with?" Willie asked. Willie was sizing them up, one of the three looked like he may be a fighter and the other two just looked as if they were trying a hand at robbing someone for the first time.

The biggest of the three spoke up, "Well sir, we was sent here by Mr. Mercurio to pick up that shine you got for him."

"Is that right," Willie answered. "And where is Mr. Mercurio?"

"He got tied up with some other things, just wanted us to bring the stuff back," the man said.

"Well that is mighty strange, seeing how Mr. Mercurio has never allowed anyone to come pick it up," Willie said. He continued, "Tell you fellows what I think. This here runt," Willie pointed at the man he had seen in the bar, "listened in on Mr. Mercurio and I when we was talking and heard our conversation. You three then got together and decided to get an easy days work by doing nothing, which in my opinion is probably what you all do. I am pretty sure work ain't in none of yawl's vocabulary."

The larger man spoke, "Well you got us figured out mister, so why don't we just make it easy and you give us the shine and your money and we won't have to leave you laying out here in the woods with that mutt."

Willie grinned and said, "Yeah I guess I could do that but see, it ain't in my nature to let a man take what I work for, especially three sorry bastards like you. I figure we got a fight on our hands and when it is over, I will take your corpse back to my place and feed them to my pet alligator and bear. That is if anything is left when Bait gets through with you."

One of the men looked at Willie and as the larger man started to step forward, he grabbed him by the arm. They stopped and the man asked, "What is your name?"

Before Willie could answer a voice came from behind the three men.

"That man is known as Willie Cane, and you fellows are lucky I got here when I did."

It was Mr. Mercurio speaking in his Italian accent. He was holding a Colt 45 in his hand and the men figured he would use it. He continued, "I should have just waited till he got finished with you but I really didn't like the thought of his gator having to eat the likes of you three then getting sick."

The men looked at each other and one said, "I have heard of you, Willie Cane - the man that lives in the swamp near Stockton."

"That would be me," Willie said.

Without another word the three men started backing away and apologizing for even thinking about robbing him. One fell backward over a piece of drift wood and the other two turned and high tailed it. Bait got a good chunk out of the leg of the one that had fell but when he got his feet under him he ran like a man with a purpose. Soon everything quieted down as the three could be heard tearing through the thick undergrowth, getting as far away as they could.

"Willie, you have a strange effect on people," Mecurio said.

"Well I sure don't mean to," Willie replied, "but I have to say you messed up a good fight. I may have had my hands full so I was thankful to hear you."

"Those three," Mercurio said, "they would have been lucky if there was anything left of them. Anyway, let's get this loaded and get out of here before they get nerve and feel like they can take us."

Willie smiled and said, "Guess you are right, we don't want to tempt them. They done and got Bait riled up now, and he gets frisky when he is riled."

Both men laughed and loaded the shine on the wagon. Mr. Mercurio headed back to town and Willie started home. He wasn't thinking about the three men or anything else. He had his mind on the gathering at the Bell's and was glad that he was going to a social gathering. It had been a long time.

Chapter 9

MEETING MISS MOLLY

Saturday could not have come quick enough. Willie grabbed some shine and jumped in the boat. He had not visited anyone on Miffin Pass in a while but he knew the Bell's place was just off of Bottle Creek. The cabin was fairly large as was the Bell family. It was a ways from the town landing and pretty much secluded. Mr. Charlie Bell had built it with his own hands and the cabin was sturdy. His wife, Lacy, and seven children worked the farm that had been cleared on some high ground near the river. Mr. Bell was a farmer that enjoyed his fishing and hunting. He liked the solitude and peacefulness of the river and the only time he wasn't home was on Sunday, when he and his family headed to church, they were a very religious family. The Bell's grew their own food and hunted for meat. They had chickens, thirty cows, two mules, several horses and some goats. The main thing Mr. Bell had was some of the best coon dogs in the country. He raised and trained them. Men would come from all around to buy one of his dogs and Mr. Bell would guarantee the dogs to be good.

As Willie neared the Bell's home he noticed several boats already there. Sam was helping with the cooking of a hog at the fire pit. Homemade banners were hung around the place congratulating Nicole for being chosen to go to college. As Willie tied the boat off on the pier, Hunter came to meet him. Willie handed the shine to Hunter knowing that Mr. Bell would not approve. Hunter told Willie to follow him to the barn where they concealed the moonshine in the hayloft. After that, Hunter took Willie down and began introducing him to the family. They met Nicole, a nineteen year old young woman with long blond hair and brown eyes. She was full of energy and greeted Willie with a hug, as she did everyone she met. She was going to the University of Alabama and study to become a doctor. A very smart young lady, Nicole planned on returning to Stockton to help take care of folks. Doctor Bettner had recommended her in a letter to the university and she was accepted.

After meeting most of the family, Willie met Mr. and Mrs. Bell and was welcomed to their home. The hog that was cooking was smelling good and there were other aromas in the air like fried chicken, apple pie and all kinds of good cooked country food. Willie would welcome a good meal since he hadn't sat down to one in quiet awhile. Several wooden tables had been placed end to end outside near two twin oaks and covered with red and white checkered table cloths. The day was pleasant, not to hot or cold. There was food from one end to the other, collard greens, chicken and dumplings, corn bread, a feast for sure. As Willie stood there admiring the foods, a young woman came out the back door of the house and the aroma caught Willie's attention but not like the woman. She had shoulder length hair, dark red and eyes as blue as the sky. Her skin was fair and soft looking and her beauty took Willie's breath. It was the woman from the funeral.

Hunter introduced her to Willie. "Willie, meet my sister Molly."

Willie stood there for what seemed an eternity looking at her. He extended his hand and she took it.

"Hi," Willie said, "I am Wi …," he didn't get his name out before Molly spoke.

"I know who you are Mr. Cane," Molly said.

All of a sudden it hit Willie, she was the little girl that had come to Doctor Bettner's office while he was getting well from the bear attack. She had changed into a woman and Willie was struck by her beauty.

Molly continued, "Have you been messing with any bears lately?"

Willie smiled and said, "No ma'am but I do have one as a pet."

Hunter had walked away to meet some other people while Molly and Willie continued their conversation.

"I know Mr. Cane," Molly said, "I know a lot of things about you," she said smiling.

"Well Miss Bell," Willie said, "if you don't mind, I wish you would call me Willie."

"I surely don't mind Willie, if you will call me Molly," she said.

"Then we got a deal," Willie said.

"Now, if you will excuse me Willie, I need to finish helping set the table," Molly said. "We will talk later."

She smiled at Willie as she walked away. She had checked him out and his rugged frame and black hair set him off as a handsome man. She would surely speak with him again before he left.

Sam walked up to Willie as she walked off.

"Well now," Sam spoke, "what you got on that mind of yours Willie?"

"I was just wondering where that beautiful woman has been," said Willie. "She has got to be one of the prettiest women I have ever seen."

"Roll up your line there a little, Willie," Sam said, "She is a fine woman but she is being courted by several men around here. You might have your hands full getting that one to step in your snare."

"Well," Willie said, "I ain't much worried about other suitor's, and I don't want to snare her, I want to marry her."

"Hold on there, Romeo," Sam snapped, "you don't know anything about her and you can't just sweep her off of her feet and run away with her. Don't know that her paw would take to kindly to that, nor her brothers,"

Willie thought about it and said, "Yeah Sam, you are right, I have to take my time. I need to lure her in and make sure she don't get away. One thing I know is that she is the woman that was suppose too come into my life. She is the one that the gypsy lady told me about."

Sam looked puzzled, "What gypsy woman?"

"The one that you told I would be coming to town the day maw died," Willie said.

"Willie, you need to rest and stay out of the sun or stop drinking that shine," Sam responded, "I ain't talked with no gypsy woman."

Willie looked at him for a second and then back at Molly.

"You sure?" Willie asked, "You didn't talk to the lady Tasha at her wagon just outside of town?"

"Man," Sam said, "I ain't seen nobody, especially a gypsy woman."

Willie scratched his head and pondered who the gypsy was and why she chose him to talk to. It didn't matter right now because so far she was right, he had a four legged friend and he felt like he had found the woman he had been seeking. He would think about this later but for now he wanted to find as much as he could about Molly.

The meal was more than everyone there could handle. After they ate, the men sat around and told stories while pitching horse shoes. The women put what food was left away and had a gathering for themselves. Willie kept his eyes on Molly every chance he could get. He would watch her as she walked and listened to her speak. Every time she would look his way, he would turn his head as if he didn't notice. In all, Willie was kind of shy but he didn't want to be, especially around her. He would wait for the right moment to talk to her.

Hunter sat down by Willie and noticed him watching Molly. He leaned over and said, "She is twenty one. She has a couple of fellows that court her every now and then but no one special."

"Why are you telling me this," Willie asked?

"Because I seen how you been watching her," Hunter said. "They want her to marry them and run away but she puts them in their place. Says she is waiting on the right man to come along and get out of this swamp. I really don't think she wants to leave here, just don't want none of them fella's that have been calling on her. I have also seen how she has been looking at you, maybe you are the man she has been looking for," Hunter said as he elbowed Willie in the side and smiled.

"You really think so," asked Willie?

"Only one way to find out, talk to her," Hunter said. "She won't bite you, Willie."

"Maybe I will," Willie said. "Maybe I will just do that, thanks Hunter."

During the afternoon the visitors were welcomed and all of them ate till they couldn't touch another bite. After everything was put away they started to mingle. Cotton had shown up with his saxophone and was well known for his musical talents with it. Hunter and his brother David played the guitar and string bass. The three got to going with some music and it all sounded great. They would play a little jazz and blues and anything else that came to mind.

Willie was sitting on the porch talking with Sam when he noticed Molly on the porch swing. He walked over to her and asked if she minded him having a seat.

"Not at all Mr. Cane, excuse me, Willie," Molly said.

"That was some mighty fine food," Willie exclaimed. "Can't say that I have ate like that in a while, everything was so good and plentiful."

Molly smiled and said, "Yes it was good and I did notice that you ate a good helping. It is good to gather like this and meet old friends and new ones."

"Yes ma'am," Willie said. "This is my first time here at your paw's place but it is real nice."

"Hunter told me he had invited you Willie and I was pleased," Molly said. "I didn't get to speak to you much at the funeral and the only other time I met you was in Doc Bettner's office, I was a lot younger as you know."

"Yeah, I remember," Willie answered, "I thought you was a pest then. It was probably because I was hurting somewhat from what that bear did to me. All I know is that you don't look anything like that now."

"I kind of got that feeling," Molly said. "You was pretty tore up that day. Anyway, that was the past and at least you are still here and now you are at my home. Strange how things work out, ain't it Willie?"

"Yeah, it is," Willie said. "I am glad Hunter asked me here, if not I wouldn't have got to see or talk with you. See, Molly, I am pretty shy and don't get around too much to get to meet a beautiful woman like you so this here has made my day."

Molly blushed a little and smiled at Willie. His heart sank some because he couldn't picture himself speaking to any woman like that but at least he got it out.

Willie continued, "I am glad I finally got to meet the pretty woman from the funeral, I had no idea who you were and didn't know how to find you."

"Thank you, Willie," Molly said, "I am flattered. Truth of the matter is Willie, I wanted to speak with you that day but maw and my paw was ready to leave. You looked handsome that day all dressed up, not like the swamp man everybody around here talks about."

"I guess I do have a reputation," Willie said. "I am not a mean man Molly, just seems like trouble sometimes finds me."

"To tell you the truth Willie," Molly exclaimed, "they don't really say that you are mean, just no one wants to mess with you because of you killing that man in Mobile. Everyone talks about you and how tough you are and how you are a legend in the swamp. I honestly feel like the folks around here like and respect you. I know Hunter does, he told paw about how you helped him catch the fish and gave him a place to stay for the night. Paw told Hunter he couldn't figure anyone better to be with because at least he was safe there."

Willie started tapping his foot on the floor and smiling. "Wasn't that much to it," Willie said, "I am sure he would have done the same for me."

"Yes, he would have," Molly replied, "for my paw to say something like that he must like you, but he may not care too much for you if he finds that shine in the barn. I told Hunter he may want to move it to the woods. Do you drink Willie?"

"Well, I will take a social drink once in a while but I have never been drunk," Willie explained. "I just don't have a taste for it and making the shine is enough for me I guess. It helps give me a little spending money, which I don't need that much. I have put back some money from that and my skinning plus my paw left me some things he said would come in handy later in life."

"How old are you Willie?" Molly asked.

"Well," Willie said, I figure to be a little over thirty, maybe thirty one." "Is my age a problem Molly?"

"No," Molly exclaimed, "not at all, I was just curious that is all. You have such a reputation and to be that young, you have had a pretty busy life."

Willie nodded and they sat and talked about many things. Molly suggested that they take a walk and Willie was more than happy to. They walked around the garden and barn then to some fields of cotton that must have been more than a hundred acres. The evening sun was beginning to fall behind the trees. They approached the house and Willie had the feeling he didn't want to leave but he knew he needed to get on down the river before dark.

"Well," Willie said, "it has been a very nice day Molly and I figure you are the cause. With that in mind, would you mind if I called on you from time to time?"

Molly smiled and said, "You can call on me whenever you like Willie. I too have enjoyed our talk and look forward to seeing you again."

Willie said his goodbye to those still there and thanked them for allowing him to come. He headed home singing. Bait had a day too as he had been playing with the other dogs and seemed tired and had laid down in the boat. When Willie began to sing, Bait joined right in, howling at the off key notes coming from Willie. The two had the song bouncing off of the cedars and it was for sure that no critter would be resting, at least until they stopped. It had been a great day for Willie and he was happy. His mind was stuck on Molly, her beauty, her voice and understanding. He had never cared for any woman or even spoken too many, but with Molly, things seemed easy. He also had not experienced the feelings he was having at this moment. He wanted to see her again and the sooner the better. He felt like he had been missing something in his life, but now maybe he had found that missing piece. Anyway, he was just going to enjoy the feelings and see what would come of it.

Molly sat on the porch thinking about Willie. She had not met a man like him and he was nothing like what she had been told. He was kind and gentle and he was very handsome. He had scars from the bear attack and other things, but from the looks of his hands, he didn't mind work and it was obvious he knew how to handle himself. She could not stop thinking about him and that was rare. Molly had been wooed by several men, none of which she had taken a serious liking too, but Willie was stuck in her mind. He wasn't like the others, he knew who he was and what he wanted in life. He never expected anything from anyone, but would go out of his way to help those that needed it. Those were good assets and she found herself interested in finding out more.

"What you thinking about sis" Nicole said. She walked over the swing and joined Molly.

"About Willie," Molly said.

"That is what I figured," Nicole said. "He is quiet handsome and nothing like what folks said him to be."

"I was thinking the same thing," Molly said.

"Well, what you going to do about it?" Nicole asked.

"What do you mean?" asked Molly.

"I mean, what are you going to do?" Nicole replied. "Molly, you have courted several fellows and it would be my guess that none of them have sparked your interest. You need to find you someone and lean towards settling down. You ain't getting no younger."

"I know Nicole," Molly said, "just don't know what to do. I want to be sure and you know how people are going to talk. They see Willie as a swamp man with no future and a lower class of a person than others."

"Wait right there sis," Nicole started, "you shouldn't let other people tell you what to do or how to think. It is none of their business who you see or what you do with your life as long as it don't interfere with them. If Willie is the one that you find yourself feeling something for, then damn it you need to make yourself happy."

Molly leaned back and looked at Nicole, she had never heard her swear or state her mind like this.

"I guess you are right," Molly said. "I need to be happy and not worry about what other folks think. Maybe I will see Willie again and get to know him better."

"Look sis," Nicole said, "I know I will be leaving here in a few days and I won't be around to take care of you. If these folks around here start giving you trouble, you just wire me and I will come take care of them for you. I will always be here for you Molly."

"Thanks Nicole," Molly said, "that is great to know and same goes here."

The girls hugged and sat talking about the day, and singing on the swing. Molly was thinking about the next time she might see Willie and how she would greet him. It would not be long because she wanted to see him and in a hurry. She didn't know him at all, but wanted to, and see what may come of it. She had to wait for now but she wouldn't wait long. There were feelings she had not experienced and she needed to know what would happen and how to deal with them. The only way to do this was see Willie and see where this would take her. The breeze on the porch was cool and the girls finally gave up and went to bed. The noises on the river seemed never ending but peaceful. The breeze picked up and heat lightning could be seen in the distance. A storm was brewing, but Molly wasn't sure if it was the weather or what her feelings for Willie might bring. Listening, Molly could hear the thunder in the distance. Her thoughts were about Willie as she closed her eyes to sleep.

Chapter 10

A DAY WITH MOLLY

Molly Bell was born in 1902 just after the turn of the century. She was the next to the oldest of the Bell children and oldest of the girls. She had a take charge type of personality and it didn't bother her to speak her mind. She wasn't afraid of work and was depended on by her mother, Lacy Bell, to help with the younger siblings of the family. She had learned the life of a farmer's daughter well and could plant seed, gather crops, can food and cook. She knew how to sew and clean house yet still didn't mind cleaning fish or an occasional deer that her paw or brothers might bring home. She was a pretty young lady and like all women her age, had dreams of going to the big city. She had been to Mobile and enjoyed the carnival season with her family but she wanted the experience of living in the city just once in her life.

Education was pretty hard to come by as the school was over eight miles from the Bell home, but she had managed to make it and learn to read and write. Since the school was such a distance from the house, the children went only three days a week. The only way to reach Stockton from where they lived was by boat and it was a twenty minute ride to landing each day. On Tuesday and Thursday's they had to stay at home and help on the farm.

When Molly finished school she got a job at the General Store in Stockton that was owned by Mr. Hymil, a Cajun from Louisiana. Mr. Hymil would tell Molly stories about New Orleans and it would make her want to go there too see it for herself. He was a true Cajun and when he spoke, Molly would have to really listen to figure out what he was saying. He lived to hunt and fish and trusted Molly with the store in his absence.

Molly arrived at the store early on that Monday morning and had not taken her mind off of the dinner or Willie. Seemed liked every time she would tell herself not to think about him, she would catch herself doing just that. Mr. Hymil had come in and told her he had to go to Mobile to pick up some merchandise for the store and would not be back until Thursday. She would need to close and open the store for the next couple of days. She told him to go ahead that she could manage, so he left on the train.

As Molly was dusting some shelves, she heard the bell on the door ring but didn't turn around as people would come and go regularly. The voice she heard made her turn around quickly and she immediately smiled.

"I need some coffee and sugar ma'am," Willie said.

"Well hello Willie," Molly exclaimed. "You startled me."

"I am real sorry about that, kind of thought that bell might have let you know someone was coming in," Willie said.

"I guess I was tied up in my work and didn't hear it," Molly replied. All the time Molly knew that she had heard the bell on the door she was just caught by surprise that it was Willie. She was wiggling out of her surprise and excitement that it was him. Molly continued, "I will get your coffee and sugar. How much did you need?"

"I need about two pounds of coffee and fifty pounds of sugar," Willie said.

"Why so much sugar, do you have a sweet tooth?" Molly asked.

"I had rather not answer that if you don't mind," Willie exclaimed. "See people already get nosey and there are some things that could get me in trouble."

"Oh, I see," Molly said. "Yeah I guess people don't need to know everything." Molly quickly figured out that he wanted the sugar to make moon shine so she didn't question him any more on it. "I will get that for you right away."

"No hurry," Willie said. "I would like to stay till dinner and take you for a bite to eat if you don't mind."

"Well Willie I don't mind at all," Molly said. "I will be closing for dinner in about twenty minutes. I sure wish you would consider changing your ways of doing some of these illegal things, Willie."

"Yeah, I plan on it," Willie said. "So far it has been good money though and hard to stop. Why Miss Bell, you need to be careful, I may think you care about my well-being."

Molly knew she needed to respond but wanted to answer him in a way that showed she was concerned about his well-being and keeping him out of trouble with the law.

"Just would hate to see you in trouble with the law, Willie," Molly said. "Especially now that we have met, I would like to get to know you better."

Molly felt like kicking herself, not knowing where those words came from. They just poured out of her mouth like water out of a bucket with a hole in it. "I mean, I mean …" Molly couldn't say anything for stuttering.

"I know what your mean, Molly," Willie said. "I am feeling the same way about you."

It placed Molly at ease a little but she needed to slow down. She kept telling herself that she needed to take it slow, but for some reason she really didn't want to. She hurried and got the coffee and sugar for Willie. He wanted to leave it there until he headed home, after they had finished their dinner. Molly locked the door to the store and they walked down the street to Kennedy's Café to eat.

The town had changed so much in the past few years. The railroad was going strong, cars were all over the place and a lot of businesses were moving out of small towns like Stockton to the bigger ones like Mobile and Montgomery. Willie grew up watching the changes and wasn't really set on all the new things going on. He liked the river and swamp, hunting, and fishing and would spend the rest of his days there, or at least try to.

The Tensaw River Delta was the second largest in the country and he hadn't been through all of it yet. Now, with this beautiful woman, he felt he may have to change some things. He didn't know what it was, but she made him think thoughts and desires he had never experienced.. As they walked to the café, he watched her and was proud to be by her side.

They talked through dinner and then Willie walked her back to the store. He grabbed his supplies and asked Molly when he would get to see her again.

"Well now, Willie," Molly said, "I guess that mostly depends on you."

"What about tonight when you close the store?" Willie asked.

"I am afraid that Hunter will be picking me up at the boat ramp and I don't have any way to get word to him," Molly said.

As they were talking, Nicole popped into the store.

"What are you doing here," Molly asked.

Nicole smiled saying, "Got to get some material, Maw wants to make me a dress for school. I told her I didn't need any more clothes, but you know Maw when she sets her mind on something. Hunter is getting some cattle feed, then we are going to wait on you to get off."

"You and Hunter can go on home," Molly said. "I will see if Mr. Cane can bring me home, that is if he wants too."

"Couldn't think of anything that I would like better, Miss Molly," Willie said with a grin.

"Great," Nicole said, "it will be good to get back home with that boat load of feed before dark anyway." She picked out some material and took out the door, looking back at Molly with a wink and big smile.

Willie grabbed the sugar and told Molly he would come back to get her at closing time. He then headed to Sam's place with the sugar. At five, Willie was back and waited until Molly locked up the store. They then walked to his houseboat.

On the way Molly talked about her desires to go to the big city just to see what it was like. She wanted to experience the people and see how they lived. She wanted to shop at the big stores and eat at fancy dinning places. She wanted to see the lights of the city and listen to the sounds of the street at night. Willie listened and asked her had she ever been to Mobile.

"Yes," Molly answered, "but I want to go to a bigger city. I would love to go to New Orleans."

"Why?" Willie asked. "What is wrong with being here in the delta and living where things are peaceful."

"It's just not the same Willie," Molly said as she placed her hand on his forearm. "See, I have been here all my life and it is all I know. I am a woman and I don't need or want fancy things, I just want to see how other people live and what goes on there. I have learned how to take care of folks, and I am sure I could take care of a husband but before I settle down and have children, I want to see that big city kind of life. Is that wrong Willie, I mean wanting to just see?"

Willie thought a second and responded, "No I don't see any harm in it Molly, but even in Mobile there is a lot of trouble, I couldn't speculate on what it would be like in a big city like New Orleans. If that is what you set your mind to then I guess that is what you need to do."

Molly smiled at Willie saying, "It can wait for now, I have other things to think about right now."

"Yeah," Willie said, "what might that be?"

Molly stopped in the middle of the road and looked at Willie, "Why that would be you Willie," she said.

She stepped up to him and placed her hands around his neck and pulled him to her. Their lips met and both knew without a doubt that this was what they had been waiting on all afternoon. After several minutes they started walking again, holding hands and talking like two love sick puppies. They could both feel the excitement of holding each other and they both knew that this would lead to other things between them.

They reached the houseboat with plenty of daylight left and Willie went inside to get a blanket for the ride down the river to the Bell's home. Molly didn't go inside because it would be frowned on if anyone saw her. It just wasn't proper even though she wanted to. Willie had just got the blanket when he heard Molly scream. He threw the blanket down and ran out the front door of the boat. He stopped dead in his tracks as he saw Molly backed up against the wall of the boat and Yam standing right in front of her. Willie decided to have a little fun and yelled at Yam. The bear turned to look at him and started walking up towards him. Bait was barking to beat the band and Yam kept coming. Willie backed off of the boat walkway and into the yard. There he stopped and got ready to tackle Yam.

Molly was telling Willie to be careful when Yam reached out and grabbed Willie and the two of them started rolling around on the ground. It looked as if they were going to kill each other then all of a sudden Molly heard Willie laughing as he now was lying across Yam and rubbing him behind his ears. Bait was tugging on Willie's pants leg and then joined Willie on top of Yam.

It hit Molly that this was the pet bear that she had heard people talk about. Feeling relieved and angry at the same time, she scolded Willie for the prank. He apologized and the next minute they were both laughing. Molly walked up as Willie explained that the bear loved to have his ear scratched and that they wrestled all the time. After some coaxing, Molly finally rubbed Yam and felt more comfortable. Willie returned inside to get the blanket and then they loaded in the boat along with Bait and headed down the river.

As they moved towards her home she listened to Willie tell about the different things on the river that they would pass. She already knew a lot of the things he was telling her but she didn't want to spoil his talking narrations, but in all the years she had been up and down this river, she didn't know that she had missed so much. Willie was smart about the delta swamp and knew it's ways. He was brave and handsome, everything a woman would want in a man. His past was not the greatest because a lot of people looked down on him for killing the man in Mobile, but then again, nobody really knew the whole story as it had changed so many times through the years.

The one thing she learned was that Willie loved a particular tree that grew on the river. It was called a Weeping Willow and was beautiful when it was green. The limbs sprouted upwards then would droop over till they almost touched the ground. She didn't know why, but he liked them and made it clear he wanted to be buried one day facing east with a Willow Tree at the head of his grave. Molly listened and made a promise to herself that she would carry out his wishes if she was around. The ride home was pleasant and she enjoyed being with Willie and listening to him talk.

Just before they rounded the bin to Molly's home, Willie stopped the boat and they embraced. After about twenty minutes, Willie cranked the motor and carried Molly safely home. As she stepped out of the boat, she was met by her father and he told her to go on in the house. Molly hesitated and he barked out the order again. Nicole had walked out to the porch and met Molly as she walked toward the house.

"Willie," Mr. Hunter started, "thank you for bringing Molly home but we can come get her. She lives here and is still my responsibility, so I will thank you to let me do what I have always done."

"Mr. Hunter," Willie said, "I ain't looking to harm your daughter. I respect you and I would never do anything to cause you or Molly any harm. I was wrong to just bring her home without your permission and I do apologize, I meant no harm."

Willie's words caught Mr. Hunter off guard. He was going to give Willie down the road, so to speak, but he never thought he would get and apology or any explanation.

"Willie," Mr. Hunter continued, "thank you for that and I can say I wasn't expecting it."

Willie found his opportunity and continued, "Mr. Hunter, I like Molly and she is a fine and beautiful woman. I would like to come courting her with your permission sir."

Mr. Hunter looked at Willie then said, "Let me ponder on it Mr. Cane. As for now though, I would like it if you would honor my wishes and only be around Molly when one of the family is with her."

Willie stood up and extended his hand to Mr. Hunter and said, "You have my word on it sir."

Molly and Nicole were still on the porch. Mr. Hunter turned to Molly and motioned her and Nicole down to the river's edge.

"Say your good byes Molly," Mr. Hunter said as he turned and walked towards the barn, "Nicole, you stay here with them."

"Yes, Paw," Nicole responded and sat down on a chair.

"I am so sorry Willie," Molly said.

"Why," asked Willie. "He cares for you and I don't have the best reputation in the world."

"Did he say we can see each other again?" Molly asked.

"Yes, as long as we have a family member with us," explained Willie.

"Will that bother you, Willie?" Molly quizzed.

Nicole butted in, "I still have three weeks, we will make sure you two get some time alone."

"Thank you Nicole," Willie said. "You ladies are lucky to have a paw like that, he reminds me of mine."

"We know," Molly exclaimed, "but sometimes he can be a little overbearing."

Willie thought a second and looked at Molly saying, "He has raised you and the others and his concerns are for your safety. He doesn't do it to be mean or control you he just wants that one thing that he has worked for so hard all these years and it is something he deserves."

"What is that, Willie," Nicole asked.

"Respect," Willie said, "Just respect for doing the best he can, not so much from you but from those like me. He wants to be sure that all of you are taken care of and the one thing he ask of men like me is just respect."

Molly and Nicole nodded in agreement and Willie said his good byes.

"I will be in touch Willie," Molly said, being corrected by Nicole,

"We will be in touch," Nicole said, smiling broadly.

"Good night ladies," Willie said, as he pushed the boat off of the bank and headed towards home.

It had been a great day and Willie had broken the ice with Molly's paw. He would be careful not to upset Mr. Bell again, but he would see Molly every chance he could. It just felt right and he knew it was meant to be.

Chapter 11

MESSAGE

MOLLY had finished the week at the store and had not seen Willie. She was feeling that her paw may have run him off. She wanted to go to the houseboat and see if he was there but she dared not because someone would surely see her. As she walked to the landing she saw a gypsy wagon sitting near the river. Hunter was not at the landing and she saw a lady sitting near the wagon. She sat on a large log and then noticed the lady at the wagon waving at her to come to her. Molly got up and walked over to the wagon.

"Hi, my name is Tasha," the lady said, her dark eyes and black hair shining from the sunlight. "You are Molly, I believe."

Molly looked puzzled, "How did you know that, how did you know my name?"

"I know a lot about you my dear," Tasha said. "I listen and I have ways of knowing things. I would like to read your palm Molly, just to see what the future holds for you."

Molly was hesitant and looked at the sign on the wagon that had prices for the readings. "I am not sure I believe in this palm reading and besides, I can't afford it. My maw and paw has always said not to believe in such things, except that we needed to be respectful of the Bible and God."

"I couldn't agree with them more," Tasha said, "I believe just as them and I know that God is for everyone and that he gave me this ability to see things and tell what may happen in the future. It is your choice, but I know there are things to come into your future and one of them already has happened."

"What might that be?" Molly asked.

"It is the man known to you as Willie," Tasha said, "There would be no charge for the reading."

Molly gazed at the gypsy and wanted to ask her how she knew but didn't. Instead she walked into the wagon with the gypsy and had her palm read. Molly listened as the gypsy told her of things that might happen. Tasha would stop at certain points of the reading and tell Molly that it was best if she didn't know the outcome. The only thing that Tasha said that made Molly feel good was that Molly would see the big city, what city she was unsure but she would go to one.

It seemed as though Molly had stayed with the gypsy for an hour but it was only a few minutes. Molly left the wagon thinking about what she had been told would happen during her life. She didn't want to believe all of it but some things did cause her to ponder what she had been told. She thanked the gypsy and walked back to the landing reaching it just as Hunter pulled up with the boat.

"What is up sis?" Hunter asked, "you look as if you have a lot on your mind."

"Hunter," Molly said inquiringly, "do you believe in the future and things coming to pass that someone predicts to happen?"

"I ain't given it much thought to tell you the truth sis," Hunter replied. "I guess there are some folks that have gifts of telling the future, but I never met one of them. Some people claim to have the gift but I pretty much don't believe that kind of stuff."

"Yeah, me either," Molly said.

"Why do you ask," questioned Hunter as he shoved the boat away from the pier and headed down the river.

"Well," Molly said, "The gypsy lady told me a lot of things was going to happen in my life and wouldn't tell me all of it, just parts of it. She knew about my life and what I wanted and some of where my life was headed."

"What gypsy lady, sis?" Hunter asked.

"The one in the wagon at the landing," Molly replied, you saw her when you pulled up."

Hunter looked back at the landing and said, "What wagon sis, there ain't no lady or wagon there. I didn't see a wagon when I pulled up, just you."

Molly looked back at where the wagon was sitting and there was nothing there. "It was there Hunter, I went inside and had my palm read and she told me my future. Where did she go Hunter?" asked Molly.

"Are you okay Molly?" Hunter asked as he was now worrying about her.

"Yeah, I'm fine," Molly replied. She was thinking about the wagon and thinking about her meeting with the gypsy. Come to think of it she didn't see any horses to pull the wagon with nor anything inside to eat. The gypsy, Tasha, had not mentioned where she was from or who she was with. Within a matter of a few minutes the wagon was gone as if it had never been there.

Molly shook her head and repeated, "I am fine."

The ride home seemed to have taken forever and Molly was quiet, not saying much. Hunter didn't say much either because he was worried about his sister and knew that something had happened at the landing. He didn't want to push it now but he would talk with Molly later after she settled down.

When they arrived home, Molly went to her room without eating. When asked about supper she told her mother she wasn't hungry. Hunter told Nicole about Molly acting strange and told her about his concerns. Nicole waited until after supper and cleaning of the dishes, then she went to Molly's room. She knocked on the door, but Molly didn't answer. She turned the door knob and opened the door scanning the room. She seen Molly sitting in a chair by the window, looking out at the river.

"Hey sister," Nicole asked, "what is going on?"

Molly never looked away from the window and said "Nothing Nicole, everything is fine."

"Not from where I am standing," Nicole responded. "Hunter told me what happened. He is worried about you and frankly, so am I."

"I wish I could tell you Nicole, but I don't know where to start or what to tell you," Molly said.

"Well, let's start with what that gypsy told you," said Nicole.

Molly turned in her chair to face Nicole. Her eyes were red and Nicole knew that she had been crying.

"What did this lady tell you?" asked Nicole.

"She only told me parts," Molly replied, "Things that she said would happen to me or might happen to me, as if I could change things by how or what I did."

"For God sake, Molly," Nicole scolded, 'what did she tell you?"

Molly started, "She said that I could bring shame to those around me, but that I would handle it the only way I knew."

"What kind of shame?" asked Nicole.

"She didn't say," Molly replied.

"What else?" Nicole said.

"She told me to follow my heart," Molly said. "She said that I would regret it if I didn't and that making the wrong choice would bring an end to someone dear to me. She said that I needed to consider my feelings and not let others choose my life for me and that I would go to the big city as I had wished."

Nicole looked at Molly and was trying to calm her feelings. Nicole said, "Molly, this lady, whoever she is, hasn't told you anything you don't already know. You will never make all the right decisions in life and some of those decisions may hurt others, but that ain't going to bring shame to you. It may hurt someone's feeling down the road, but not because you don't make the right decisions. Decisions are choices Molly, and choices are decisions that have not been made. Hunter said he didn't see the gypsy or the wagon so maybe you just fell asleep at the landing and dreamed this stuff."

"No Nicole," Molly said, "it was real as day. That wasn't all she told me, she said that my life would be made happy and sad by my actions and that in the end I would find death a wish for me."

"That is crazy stuff Molly," Nicole replied. "My suggestion is that if you see this gypsy again, you ignore her and go the opposite direction." "I still believe you were dreaming this stuff so let's forget about it and let life take us where it will."

Molly nodded and said, "Maybe your right."

"Of course I am right," Nicole said. "Hey, Maw cooked up a black berry pie and it was sure good. Want to go down and eat a bite then have some of that pie with cream."

"Sure," Molly said, "I am kind of hungry. You are right sister, maybe I did fall asleep and dream all this stuff. I hope that is what happened anyway because I would sure hate to think I saw a ghost. People would really have something to talk about then."

"Don't you be worrying about all that stuff," Nicole said. "Let's go get you some supper and don't think about it anymore."

The two hugged each other and went down stairs to the kitchen to get Molly some food. They ate their pie and the two went out on the porch and set in the swing.

"When are you going to see Willie again?" asked Nicole.

"Hopefully soon," Molly answered. "I think he will be at the County Fair this weekend and I will get to see him. I haven't heard from him in a week, I was kind of hoping paw didn't scare him off."

"Did you say the County Fair?" asked Nicole.

"Yes," replied Molly, "why?"

"All I can say, sister," Nicole exclaimed, "is cotton candy. I love cotton candy and I am going to get all I can eat of it."

After sitting and talking awhile the girls were joined by their maw. They all made plans to carry canned foods to the fair as well as cakes and pies for judging. Mr. Bell was carrying two prize bulls and some young calf's to be judged in the cattle competition. He usually won because he had raised some of the best beef in the county, if not Alabama. Maw was well known for her pies and preserves and the girls had won ribbons in making dresses and such. In all it looked to be a fun day for the whole family and especially for Molly. She was looking forward to seeing Willie. He had not left her mind for a minute and she couldn't wait to see him.

After their maw had gone to bed, the two girls sat for a while longer and talked about things. Nicole wanted to make sure that Molly was okay and things were back to normal even though she felt that something had happened at the landing.

They both laughed and Molly felt a little easier about things, but she was not ready to forget what she knew without a doubt had happened. It was in her head and she had deep feeling that this gypsy was right, but she didn't know who the gypsy was talking about or how to handle her life to make sure things were right. The only thing that the gypsy said was it was fate and what ever happened was meant to be.

It was late as the girls finally decided to call it a night. As Molly climbed into bed her thoughts were of the gypsy and of Willie. She hoped to never see the gypsy again, but could not wait to see Willie. As she closed her eyes, she saw Willie and carried him into her dreams.

Chapter 12

A FAIR DELIGHT

Willie had finished early from his trapping and was cleaning up around the houseboat when Sam came through the door. It had been a while since Sam had stopped by because his wife had just bore their seventh child. He had been staying around helping her get things settled with all them children and he was sure glad to get away for a while.

"What's been happening, Willie?" Sam asked.

Willie looked at Sam and smiled answering, "Not much, been trapping some up around Bates Lake and Otter Bayou near McIntosh. It is a ways up there, so I been camping out up that way for four and five days at a time. The trapping is real good though. Now, what brings you this way?"

"Well," Sam started, "I have been stuck at the house with them heathen children, seems like forever and the wife told me to go relax, she was feeling better and could handle things, me being the good husband and all. So I just come by to see if you wanted to run over to the fair and check out the free samples of food and see what is going on there."

"I don't know, Sam, I have a lot of things that need mending and I really don't have the time," Willie said.

"Come on, Willie," Sam pleaded, "if you don't go I will get myself in trouble with one of them young girls frolicking around there and then my wife will have something to fuss about."

Willie smiled knowing that Sam would never think of fooling around on Sarah. They were childhood sweethearts and there was no woman that would ever take her place with Sam.

"Is it that Sam," Willie asked grinning, "or is it that you have taught that woman how to shoot and you know she might be shooting off some of your body parts if she caught you?"

Sam laughed, "Yeah, that too. Anyway, come on and lets go, I hear that Molly will be there too, that should interest you."

Willie looked at Sam and grinned. "Well," Willie said, "maybe you're right, I probably do need to take a break and see what they got at the fair. Besides, I sure would like to see her, it has been a spell and I been thinking about her a lot."

"Well come on then, they got a rodeo going on and a horse race, I would like to bet on," exclaimed Sam.

Willie walked inside and got his hat, then the two men headed off towards the fair. As they got into town they spotted Mr. Hymil loading his flat bead truck. All these motor run vehicles had never appealed to Willie, with the exception of the motor for his boat. They were loud and some of them smoked but Willie knew this was called progress and it seemed that everyone was getting them.

"Where you fellows headed?" asked Mr. Hymil.

"Going to the fair and catch that rodeo and horse race," Sam replied.

"Well if you two want a ride, I would be glad to give you one as soon as I am finished loading up," Mr. Hymil said.

"Mighty kind of you," Willie said. Sam and Willie walked over and helped Mr. Hymil load the truck with merchandise from the store that he would sell at the fair. It was a good five miles to Bay Minette where the fair was being held, so the ride would help them out. They jumped onto the back of the truck and Mr. Hymil pulled off.

The ride was bumpy with the dirt roads being washed out a little by the rains but it didn't take that long. After arriving they helped Mr. Hymil unload the truck. He told them when he would be heading back to Stockton and they agreed to return and help him load up and catch a ride back. The two men then starting roaming around checking out the fair.

They headed toward the arena and stood at the end of the fence watching the bull riding. It was pretty rank as these riders would hold their hand in the air and come out of a thing called a chute holding onto a rope wrapped around the belly of that bull. If the rider could hold on for eight seconds then he would be scored. The ride was rough. If the rider fell off, a fellow with his faced painted up would come in and distract that bull until the rider or cowboy, as he was called, could reach safety, usually on the fence. The clown or bull fighter, saved a lot of the cowboy's bacon that day as they were hitting the ground pretty regularly.

Sam and Willie watched for a while and were fixing to look around some more when a rider came out of the chute on a big gray looking bull called DR, short for the Doctor.

That bull had horns and in the middle of those horns was one mad animal. The cowboy made the eight seconds but then he had to get off that critter. When he hit the ground that bull spun around so fast that he nailed that cowboy in the britches sending him about twelve feet in the air. The clown moved in to try and save the rider and then that big bull found himself with two men to play with. That bull caught the clown and chucked him right beside the rider that had just landed, and both those fellas were in that bull's sights.

He was on top of those two men so fast that neither could move, and he was rolling them around on the ground. The crowd was standing and yelling for someone to help the men. It didn't take anyone long to realize that the bull intended on hurting both those men.

Willie jumped that fence and ran straight at that bull. Sam yelled at Willie but it was too late. Willie reared back and when he reached that bull, he struck the animal as hard as he could behind the ear. The bull staggered and went sideways from the blow. He spun and looked at Willie. Willie stood there and the big bull snorted and pawed the ground. As if he knew what the bull was thinking, Willie started speaking to that animal.

"Now look here fella," Willie said. "It is best for you to take yourself on back to the pen and eat some hay. You have put on a show for all these folks, but these two fellows here are trying to make a living and they feed you for what you do. If you come back at me, or them, then you and I will have big problems and in the end you will end up on somebody's plate. Now get on out of here."

The two men on the ground had gotten to their feet

and were headed for the gate. They both would survive but needed to get some medical attention. The bull stared at Willie and realizing that he had met his match, turned away and trotted back towards the gates leading to his pen. He turned his head back once before going through the gate, looking at Willie who was still standing there. As the bull walked through the gate and out of the arena the crowd began to clap. In all the emotions, Willie had acted without thinking and probably saved those two men from severe injury and possible death.

Sam just stood there gazing at Willie. "You are without a doubt either the bravest, or dumbest, man I have ever met," Sam exclaimed as Willie climbed back over the fence.

The bull fighter walked up to Willie and thanked him for saving the two men from the bull. "Sir," the clown said, "that was the wildest thing I have ever seen. You are either nuts or pure damn crazy, but I thank you for helping us out. That bull pretty much had us where he wanted us and if you hadn't of stopped him, he may have killed us. DR is the meanest that I have ever had to fight and I usually just get up on the fence after the rider is safe and let him stalk around in pride. He has hurt a few cowboys in his time. Again, thanks for your help."

Willie shook the clowns hand and said he was glad they were okay. People were still applauding as Willie and Sam started to leave the area. As they neared the end of the arena, Mr. Bell walked up to Willie.

"That was one of the bravest things I have ever witnessed, Mr. Cane," Mr. Bell said. "That is the meanest bull around and you stopped him dead in his tracks. My compliments, Willie," Mr. Hunter said, "well done."

Willie didn't have the heart to tell any of them that his knees were weak and all he wanted to do was sit down. The word had spread fast throughout the fairgrounds as to what had happened. Again Willie had brought attention to himself, but this time it was good. As Sam and he walked, they came across Nicole coming from one of the vendors. She had two wads of cotton candy, one pink and one blue.

"Hey Willie," Nicole said smiling, "heard what you did at the arena. Pretty brave of you saving those two men like you did."

"It wasn't nothing, really," Willie replied. "Where is Molly?"

"She is in the canning tent with Maw while they are judging," Nicole said as she pointed towards the tent.

"You want me to carry her that cotton candy?" Willie asked.

"Shoot no," Nicole responded, "this ain't for her, these are mine. She don't care much for it so I am eating her part too."

Willie smiled, "You going to get a belly ache from all that sugar."

Nicole took a big bite and smiled, saying, "Yeah, probably so, but it is so good."

Sam left to go bet on the horse race and Nicole walked with Willie to the canning tent. As they entered, Willie spotted Molly standing next to her mother. Nicole walked up behind Molly and stuck a wad of cotton candy in her face. Molly leaned back and threw her hands up laughing at Nicole. As she turned she saw Willie and her expression changed to that of a little girl on a play-ground. She shyly bowed her head and greeted him. Mrs. Bell also turned around and spoke to Willie and smiled.

"We have heard about what you done Mr. Cane," Mrs. Bell said. "That was very brave of you."

"I am not real sure if it was brave or dumb to tell you the truth," Willie replied. "I just did it without thinking much on it. If I had time to think about it I probably would have chosen a different way."

"Either way," Mrs. Bell said, "you helped those men out and that was what mattered."

"What is happening here?" Willie asked.

"They are getting ready to announce the ribbon winners for canned jellies," Molly said. "Maw is in the running this year for strawberry jam." She lost out to Mrs. Hooper last year, but Maw has changed her recipe."

They stood watching as the judges walked out to the jars of preserves sitting on the tables. Within a few minutes they and finished and ribbons placed on the winners. Mrs. Bell took first place in strawberry, blackberry and pear jams. She also won the blue ribbon in her Coconut Cake and Egg Custard pie. It was her best year and she was smiling, trying not to look like she was all full of herself.

After the contest, Molly and Willie started walking around looking at the games and other things going on. Mr. Bell had won the Best in Show for his prize bull and had sold three calves. A fence surrounded the fair and the two strolled out a nearby gate and into a shaded area in a clump of trees. They sat down with a cool breeze blowing on them.

The sounds of the fair were blocked out by the beating of their hearts, and their kisses were passionate. Willie had never been with a female like Molly and she had never been with a man. Her urges were strong and she found herself wanting to go further with him than she had any of the other men she had been around. Willie could feel every curve on her body next to his and he had to keep telling himself to wait. They both knew that it would be special and they also knew that they would have to wait for the right time and place to share the feelings they were having.

After about thirty minutes they agreed it was time to go back to the fair and join the family. The sun was going down and it was beginning to get late. Molly rejoined her maw and paw. She helped them start packing their wares. Sam had made it back and was helping Mr. Hymil load the truck.

Willie helped the Bell's get their stuff loaded and was saying his goodbyes when Hunter walked up. Hunter told Mr. Bell that the man that had purchased the livestock had to leave and wanted the cattle brought to Selma within the week He would pay an extra one hundred dollars for their delivery. Mr. Bell agreed to have the cattle there by Thursday and Hunter was sent to tell the man of the agreement.

Molly turned and whispered to Willie, "They will be gone for three days. Can you see me Wednesday after work?"

"Sure I can," Willie responded, "Couldn't think of nothing I would like better."

Molly smiled at Willie and walked away smiling back at him. Willie shook Mr. Bell's hand in parting. Sam and Mr. Hymil had finished loading the truck and they all loaded up and headed back to Stockton. It had been a very busy, interesting and enjoyable day, with the exception of the bull. The time Willie had spent with Molly was worth the trip and he thanked Sam for tricking him into coming.

Sam looked at Willie saying, "Man you need to be careful with that girl. She is pretty and all but her paw ain't one to be messing with if you know what I mean."

"Don't worry Sam," Willie said, "I have no intentions of upsetting Mr. or Mrs. Bell. Molly is a beautiful woman and I will treat her with respect, but you mark my words Sam, I will make her my wife one day."

"I have no doubt about it Willie," Sam replied. "I am just warning you, Mr. Bell ain't no bull, he will come back at you again and again if he feels you are messing up with his daughter. Just you be careful."

"Thanks Sam," Willie said, "I will be."

The ride home was quiet and Willie's only thoughts were about Molly. It was a good day, now he would have to wait until Wednesday before he could see her again. What would happen then he did not know, but he did know that whatever happened he was going to enjoy it because he would be with Molly.

Thinking back about the bull, Willie couldn't explain why he did what he did. He saw two men in trouble and he just reacted to their needs. He never thought about being injured or being afraid. When he struck the bull he knew it wouldn't kill the animal but Willie had spent his whole life around wild animals and he knew that being afraid was dangerous and a sign of weakness. The bull knew that it was time to move on back to the safety of his pen. It was probably the first time the bull had been challenged and somehow that bull knew that this person wasn't like the two laying on the ground.

Willie knew that he would need to heed Sam's words and be aware of Mr. Bell so as not to upset him. He already respected the man, but he was sure he felt like the bull did today. He knew there would be a time when he would need to go about his business and give respect where it was due. Willie had found the woman he had searched for all these years, now he had to be brave and show no fear yet be respectful, just as he had done today. He could do it and he would.

Chapter 13

LOVE IN THE SWAMP

Molly worked hard the start of the week and waited on Wednesday. Her thoughts were completely on Willie and dreams of him kissing her. It was late on a Wednesday afternoon and Molly was getting excited. She told her maw she would be seeing some of the ladies for a sewing bee and would be after dark getting home. Of course she knew her Maw would be worried, but Molly had traveled the river many nights by herself and this night the moon would be full and she felt safe.

About ten minutes before closing three young women walked in and Molly could hear them talking. Word had spread around that Molly had been seen at the fair with Willie. The town of Stockton wasn't that big so it didn't take long for gossip to get going. Molly was dusting shelves and could hear the three women talking. They acted as though they didn't know Molly was there.

"Have you heard what Willie Cane done at the fair, saving those men from that bull?" the youngest women asked.

A second woman replied, "Hear it, I watched it! He leaped over that fence and struck that bull right between the eyes. That bull was stunned and just walked off."

The third woman then began to speak, "Yeah, he is a strong looking and handsome man, but I wouldn't want to be caught with him."

"Why not?" one of the women asked.

"He is a swamp man," the third woman replied. "Could you imagine having to live on that old houseboat and smell all those animals he has around there." "It would be a miserable life for any woman, having to live like a hermit. The man is caught in the past and as far as I can tell has just recently got electricity. He don't have a car or no way to get around, not even a horse. It would be an awful way to live."

The three ladies rambled on for some time and Molly just listened. They knew she was the one with Willie at the fair and they were gossiping in their own way and hoping she would hear their conversation. Molly heard it but she didn't let it change her mind about Willie. She was content with her decision to be around him and besides, over half of her life she had been without the finer things in life. Her paw didn't have a car either but they made do with what they had.

Soon the three ladies left and Mr. Hymil told Molly to lock the store up. She finished the day's receipts and was soon on her way. She climbed into the boat and headed towards Willie's houseboat. After about a five minute ride up the river the houseboat came into view. Her heart started pounding and she began to think of how this would look to folks. She knew in her mind it was wrong, but she also knew that she cared for Willie and kept telling herself over and over this was the right thing for her. She was twenty-two and most women had already married by the age of eighteen. She had waited for the right man and she felt that Willie was that man.

After securing the boat she started up the ramp to the porch. There was a wonderful smell coming from inside. Just as she reached the door it opened and Willie greeted her and asked her to come in. As she stepped inside, she found the houseboat to be clean and tidy. It looked as though Willie had spent all day cleaning the place up. Bait was laying on a deer rug in the corner and lifted his head as she came in.

"What is that wonderful smell?" asked Molly.

"That is some rabbit stew," Willie said. "It has carrots, peas and potato's in it. I also have some rice cooked and baked a sweet potato pie. I hope you like stew."

Molly stood there for a moment and looked at Willie. "Where did you learn to cook?"

"My maw felt like I should learn so she taught me after my paw died," Willie responded. "I can cook just about anything," he said as he was taking some corn bread out of the wood stove.

"Molly smiled and said, "I love stew and I am very impressed."

"That is what I am here for," Willie said, grinning.

Molly sat down at the table which was adorned with a half burned candle and some wild daisies in an old glass bottle. The table cloth had been cleaned and smelled of the fresh outdoors. Willie had electricity but he wanted the night to be special and had lit an old kerosene lantern which gave off a soft glow. Molly liked all of it and the romantic feelings that the room set off. She knew Willie had spent the day getting ready and she was happy to see that he did have a romantic side to him. She helped him set the table with some very nice china which had been saved by his maw. They then sat and ate the meal that had been prepared and she found the stew to be outstanding. Her biggest surprise was the sweet potato pie. It was as good as any she had tasted. Willie was full of surprises and his cooking for a swamp man wasn't bad at all.

Willie had not stopped smiling and after they had eaten their supper, he cleaned the dishes and asked Molly if she would like to go for a walk. It was still early and the sun was just beginning to set. They walked through the trails and down by the river, enjoying the sounds of the animals. It was a time when the animals would prepare for night, with the owls coming out searching for food. Turkey and deer would be settling in for the night with the turkeys flying to the trees for protection from predators. Coyotes could be heard yelping in the swamp as they gathered their packs and began to hunt for unsuspecting victims like rabbit, young deer and hogs. Owls would screech and carry on, calling to each other in a mating ritual that would go on for hours. Frogs and gators would also began to make noises tuning in to the night sounds of the crickets and locust. It sounded like a symphony of the wild and could only be experienced in the swamp.

After their walk, Willie and Molly returned to the houseboat. They talked for a long time as they sat on the porch and spoke of things going on in their lives. It was now dark and the moon began to peak above the cypress.

"It is getting late Molly, and I wouldn't feel comfortable with you traveling that river at night by yourself," Willie said.

"I am a big girl Willie, I can take care of myself," Molly replied.

"You haven't seen some of the things I have seen on this river," Willie replied. "Some things that have even put a fear in me."

"Not you," Molly exclaimed, "not the famous Willie Cane. I don't think anything scares you."

"You do," Willie said. "You scare me Molly, I ain't never met a woman like you."

Willie was standing by the gang plank and Molly stood up and walked over to him.

"Why Willie," Molly said, "you don't have to be afraid of me. I am a river rat just like you. I may not get in the swamp and trap and fish like you but I have lived here all my life and with my family we have survived. You have a reputation and people have made things of it, some good, some bad, but they don't know you Willie. They have not met the man I am standing here with and they form opinions which are wrong. I shouldn't scare you Willie, we are alike in a lot of ways."

Willie looked into her eyes and smiled. He leaned over and kissed her and Molly knew that this was where she wanted to be right now. They embraced for what seemed like an eternity. Their kisses were meaningful and there was no doubt both of them knew what they wanted.

After several minutes Willie looked at Molly and said, "I really will worry about you on that river, you should probably go and get home before it gets too late."

Molly looked at Willie and said, "Perhaps you are right." She turned to walk down the plank.

Willie hated to tell her to leave, but he wanted things to

be right and not act like a wild man. He lowered his head and turned toward the door when her heard Molly's voice.

"Willie," Molly said, "I never been with a man before, but I would really like to stay awhile."

Willie turned towards her. She was still facing away from him and turned as he started to speak.

"Are you sure?" Willie asked.

"Yes," Molly answered.

Willie reached out and took her by the hand. They walked into the houseboat and closed the door behind them. As they entered the bedroom Willie closed the door with Bait still lying on the rug, watching them. Willie picked Molly up and gently laid her on the bed. No words were spoken. After several minutes they both removed their clothes and eased under the covers.

All of Molly's fears were gone. Willie's hand were rough, but his touch was gentle. He rubbed his hands over Molly's body and she could feel the excitement growing inside her. The evening was one she would never forget. Willie was gentle and calm, his voice soothed her and the moments were not wasted. He did not force her, he let her control the situation and she enjoyed every moment of it. It was the most wonderful experience she had ever been through and she was not ashamed or sorry that it happened. She was especially not ashamed to be with Willie. He was gentle, kind and caring, more than she had ever imagined.

After a few hours, Molly left the houseboat and went home. Willie was standing on the bank of the river watching her as she rounded the bend of the river disappearing from site. Making love to Molly was what he had pictured for several months. Now what would happen, what would this do to their relationship? Would things change between them or would they grow closer? All he knew was that Molly had changed his mind about ever being with a woman and he was liking the way it felt. He started whistling and Bait picked up his ears and turned his head sideways, looking at Willie. It was if Bait thought they were fixing to go out hunting and he stood up wagging his tail.

Willie looked at Bait and said "Come on fella, let's go get us a couple of coons. The night is still young and they should be feeding down by Hastie." Willie grabbed his gun and the two started off into the night. Willie knew he wouldn't be able to go to sleep so he would just hunt. It would tire him out so he could sleep later. Three coons later and with dawn breaking, Bait and Willie made it back to the houseboat and after cleaning their kill, went off to sleep. The sun had warmed things up and it was just plain comfortable. Willie closed his eyes and fell off to sleep, dreaming of Molly.

Molly woke up with Nicole sitting on the side of her bed. Nicole had that look on her face.

"Do you know what time it is sis? asked Nicole.

"No," answered Molly, "what time is it?"

"It is past nine and you were supposed to have went to work this morning." Nicole said.

Molly jumped up looking startled and started grabbing her clothes.

"It is okay, I had Hunter stop by and tell Mr. Hymil you was ill so he wouldn't be expecting you today."

"Thank you," Molly said. "I must have been tired."

"I am sure you were," Nicole said, grinning.

"What do you mean by that?" Molly asked.

"Oh nothing but that you looked all chipper and giddy

last night when you got home and your hair was a little messed up." Nicole said, still grinning. "Want to fill me in on how things went with you and Willie?"

"No I do not," Molly said. "It is none of your business." Molly was smiling as she tried to keep a straight face. "All I can tell you is that we had a very nice evening."

"Sure was," exclaimed Nicole, "nice enough to make you sleep late. Anyway, when are you going to see him again?"

"I am not sure," Molly answered. "I hope it won't be too long." Inside Molly was happy and anxious. She had never felt this way and it was a feeling of joy and longing. A joy of being with Willie and a longing to see him again soon, very soon.

Molly finished getting dressed and she and Nicole went to Stockton. She went to the store and apologized to Mr. Hymil telling him the truth about her over sleeping. He said he understood and told her to take the day off. He asked if she would tend the store for a few days while he went to New Orleans. She agreed to do it and then she and Nicole went shopping. She was happy, not that she hadn't been smiling before, but now she couldn't seem to stop.

Nicole saw it too and looked at her saying, "Funny how things can change overnight in a person."

"What are to talking about?" Molly asked.

"You know, sis," Nicole answered. "I mean how full of life and energy a person gets when something special happens to them."

"Give me an example, Nicole," Molly said, "what are you blabbering about?"

Nicole grinned again and said, "Like when a lady finally becomes a woman."

Molly looked at her and dropped her head a little as if she was shy or embarrassed.

Nicole continued, "Not to worry, sis, it happens and with you I must say, I am glad to see it."

The two girls looked at each other and Molly hugged Nicole.

"Don't know what I would do without you sis," Molly said.

"Sure you do, Molly," Nicole responded. "You would do just fine."

The two sisters spent the rest of the day enjoying each other's company and Molly continued to dream of Willie and waited for her next time to see him.

Chapter 14

STRANGE PARTING

Over the next several months Willie and Molly continued their secret relationship, but it wasn't as secret as they thought. Nicole had left for Tuscaloosa and Molly found herself wishing for Nicole's company. It would have been nice to have someone to talk to about her adventures with Willie and the feelings that she had been sharing. Molly had found the time to spend with Willie and they had traveled the swamp enjoying the serenity and peacefulness of it all. Willie knew everything about it, the trees, animals, river current and how the moon phased disrupted the tide. He was a hard worker and when it came to compassion he knew how to treat a woman. Molly was content in his arms and missed him when she was away from him, but she felt a need to hide it from others. Willie didn't understand, but he had fallen in love with her and never questioned her about it.

Molly had heard people talk about Willie and she wanted to speak up but was afraid to say anything. She wanted to tell them he was not as they thought, but that he was a kind and gentle man with a big heart. Every time something stopped her and she couldn't find the words. She kept telling herself she would let people know and in time she would, just not now.

After about five months of meeting secretly Willie had decided to ask Molly to marry him. He had gone to town, and on the same day he purchased a pick-up truck he bought a ring for her. The truck was his first and Sam had to teach him how to drive it. Trapping was no longer the best way to make a living and he had to change his methods of making money. His moonshine still made money but he always felt that he would get caught sooner or later. He had turned to fishing for catfish and would sell them to the fish markets in Bay Minette and Mobile. It was easier to drive to the markets than to travel by river so he learned how to drive the truck. He planned to ask her when she came by the houseboat that night.

As Willie waited that evening there was a stillness in the air. He had cooked up some fried chicken, collars and made potato salad. He had placed a candle on the table. Bait stood up and the hair on the back of his neck stood up. Willie could hear the soft footsteps and watch as the door come open. Molly walked in and stood in the doorway. She looked at Willie and it was obvious she had been crying. Willie walked over to her and reached to hold her but Molly stepped back.

"What is wrong, Molly?" Willie asked.

"Willie," Molly said, "I have to tell you something." Molly scanned the room as if she was looking for something to say and saw the small jewelry box sitting near the candle on the table. She broke into tears and said, "Oh Willie, I don't know how to say this. I have to leave the swamp. I am moving to New Orleans and I won't be back for a while."

Willie looked at her and lowered his head. He didn't know what to say. His heart had sunk into his stomach and he felt as if all the blood had been drained from him. He wanted to ask her why, what had happened but he couldn't speak.

Molly continued, "I have a chance to visit the big city Willie, to see how it is to live there and if I don't like it then I will come back. Please don't hate me Willie, please don't."

Willie slowly walked past her and out the door. He walked down the ramp and over to the bank of the river. His heart was broken because on this night he wanted the woman he loved to answer a question, one that he now would not ask. He sat down on the bank and Bait came and sat beside him. He did not look back at Molly

Molly cried as she walked over to the table and picked up the tiny box. She opened it and saw the beautiful ring, sitting down in a chair, she wept as she called his name, "Oh Willie, my truest love, Willie". She set the box on the table and walked out of the houseboat. She watched Willie sitting on the bank, his silhouette outlined by the moon. She wanted to go down to him but she couldn't. She walked away into the darkness.

Willie sat on that bank till almost morning. He had never shed a tear but on this night he had cried more than he thought any man should have. He gathered himself up, loaded his boat, and with a heavy heart he and Bait headed out to run lines and catch some fish.

Four days past and the pain in Willie's heart was so severe that he hadn't eaten much or felt like doing anything. He had left the box on the table and not once thought about taking it back. After the fourth day, Willie could not stand it anymore and he headed toward the Bell place to see Molly. He had to know why she really left. He didn't believe that the big city was all she left for and he wanted to talk to her, that was all, just talk.

As he landed the boat, he walked up the bank and was met there by Mrs. Bell.

"Good evening Mrs. Bell, is Molly home?" Willie asked.

"No Willie," Mrs. Bell said, "She left yesterday, headed to New Orleans." "Is there something you wanted to talk to her about?"

Willie pondered a minute and said, "Yes ma'am but I guess it is too late now. Seems like my life story Mrs. Bell, you have a good day."

Willie turned and started walking towards the boat when Mrs. Bell spoke.

"She loved you Willie, and it hurt her to leave, but if I know anything about Molly, she loved you."

Willie turned around to look at her and asked, "Then why Mrs. Bell, why did she leave?"

"I guess you will have to ask her when she comes back Willie," Mrs. Bell exclaimed. "She has some things she wanted to work out and she will come back. When she does, she will explain everything to you and you two can have the life you want."

Willie looked down at the ground and said, "Thank you Mrs. Bell for telling me that, wish I could feel the same as you."

"She will be back Willie," Mrs. Bell said again. "She will be back."

Willie looked at Mrs. Bell and she was crying. It was as if she wasn't really sure that Molly would be back either and

Willie felt that not only had he lost the woman he loved, but that Mrs. Bell had lost her daughter. Willie got into his boat and headed down the river. Things felt as though they were so far away and Willie didn't know how to get them back into sync. All he wanted was to be alone. He wanted no one around and he didn't want to talk, he just wanted time to think.

As Willie neared his houseboat he saw Sam sitting on the porch. He pulled up and tied the boat off. As he stepped up on the houseboat Sam got up from the rocker and greeted him.

"What is up, my friend?" Sam asked.

Willie didn't feel like talking but Sam was his friend and knew everything about Molly and him. "Nothing much Sam," Willie replied.

"Hum," Sam sighed, "then why the long face and the look of sadness?"

"I really don't to talk about it Sam," Willie said.

"Don't have to my friend, seen the ring box on the table and I know Molly left yesterday, don't take much to figure things out," Sam exclaimed.

"I don't know what happened Sam," Willie explained. "I thought everything was going fine and we both felt the same. She just up and left, said she wanted to see what the big city was like."

"Well," Sam started, "I would like to tell you I know about women and how they think, but the truth is I learn something new nearly every day. I've been married over twenty years and got seven kids, and I can't tell you from one day till the next what that woman is thinking. Seems like she can change her mind at the drop of a hat, you just never know what goes on in their mind."

Willie looked and Sam and just shook his head.

"Tell you something else Willie," Sam continued, "Molly will come back. She may find out she don't like the city stuff and she will be back here in the swamp before you know it."

"Second time I heard that today," Willie said, "just don't seem to help what I am feeling."

"Paw told me it will ease with time, Willie," Sam said. "He was always pretty good with that kind of guidance."

"Why are you here Sam?" Willie asked.

"Can't come visit a friend," Sam said. Sam knew that Molly had left and he also knew that Willie would be hurting. He had to have a reason so he asked Willie for some help. "I need your help, Willie."

"What on heavens for, you have seven kid's, can't get them to help you?" Willie questioned.

"Not with this," Sam said. "I have an order for seventy five gallons of shine and I need some help cooking and transporting it."

Willie thought for a second and said, "Okay, guess going to jail right now wouldn't be so bad since I really don't have anything else holding me back."

"Don't be talking like that, Willie," Sam said. "You going to jinx us right off the bat. I will come by and pick you up in the morning. We need to get an early start and it will be a walk to the steel. Got it hid up near Douglas Lake."

"I will see you then, Sam," Willie exclaimed.

Sam turned and started to walk off but Willie stopped him.

"Thanks, Sam," Willie said.

"For what?" Sam asked.

"For being the best friend a man could have and knowing when I need to talk."

Sam grinned real big and said, "Willie don't go getting mushy on me now, I got enough kids that do that. You are my friend and if I was in your shoes, you would do the same for me. Get some sleep Willie, we need to get an early start."

Sam left and Willie finished skinning the catfish for market. He cleaned up the houseboat and picked up the box that had the ring in it. He walked over to a wooden box that he kept money and other articles in, putting the small box in the larger one. As he started to close it, Willie stopped. He set the box back on the table and picked up the small ring box again. In his hand he held what he hoped would be his life's dream of a spouse that he would love and cherish. He opened the box and stared, his eyes watering up a little as he looked at an empty box.

What did it mean, why did she take the ring? When would she return? All these questions were going through Willie's mind. He had no answer, but he knew he must wait and he felt that it would be the hardest thing in the world to do. She was gone for now and his heart was in his throat because he didn't know why. Either way he would wait for her. It was not that he had to or that anyone told him to. It was because he loved her and he knew he would not be happy with anyone else. He would wait, it was all he could do if he wanted to be with Molly. He would wait because she had taken his heart and he didn't know what else he could do. It was heartbreak, something he had never felt before and hoped to never feel again. Yes, Willie would wait.

Chapter 15

SOME TIME AWAY

Molly looked down at the ring on her finger. She had left the swamp five years ago and she had worn the ring every day since she had left. The big city wasn't what she had believed it would be. Nothing was as she thought it would be especially the hurt that had come when she left the Tensaw River Delta. She walked out of the bakery she had worked at for the past few years and headed down the crowded streets towards her small one room apartment. As she walked she looked at homeless people begging for anything that a person would give them. Hobos and wino's huddled together drinking cheap wine, some passed out from too much to drink. Others just standing around barrels with fires burning from whatever wood could be scrapped up. For some it was all the warmth they could find and for some the last heat they would feel in this life. Times had become very hard and to make a living for a family was almost impossible. Just to survive took everything a man or woman could do.

Molly walked to the City of New Orleans Orphanage and was met at the door by the keeper, Mr. Jamison Roland.

Mr. Roland was a kind generous man and believed in taking care of the children that had been abandoned. Unlike other orphanages, there was a real care for the children and the people that worked here treated the children with respect and kindness. The children liked it there, they received food, clothes and an education which Mr. Roland felt was necessary if they would exceed in the world. Most of the workers in the orphanage had been orphans themselves and had stayed there to help take care of the children that had been brought there. Mr. Roland greeted Molly as she stepped in the door.

"Good afternoon Molly," Mr. Roland said." "Hope your day went well." He summoned one of the workers, "Bring Janine up here please." The worker headed off to the back of the dorm.

"I am fine sir," Molly replied. "It is a little cold out today, but I think I have enough coal to keep us warm tonight."

"If not Molly, I will bring up a bucket for you. We have just received a new load this afternoon," responded Mr. Roland.

"I would appreciate that Mr. Roland, you are so kind, thank you." exclaimed Molly.

"If Mrs. Roland found out I didn't help you, she would be very angry, and I would end up cold and sleeping on the couch."

They both laughed and Mr. Roland walked out the back door carrying a coal bucket. In a few moments he returned placing the bucket by the door.

"How are things going at the bakery?" Mr. Roland asked.

"Oh things are very slow, no one has money to buy

much so it has not been very good," Molly said. "Mrs. Nan is hoping it will pick up, but I just don't know." "Everything is bad Mr. Roland, people are starving and there is not much work." "Sometimes I feel it would be better if I went home, at least there I knew how to get food and what to do."

About that time the door opened and the small girl walked in and ran to Molly giving her a hug. The girl was around five years old and had plum red hair and dark eyes. She was wearing the dress that all children at the orphanage wore, kind of a faded blue. She had a small coat and quickly put it on.

"I am so glad to see you Ms. Molly," the little girl said. "Will I be here tomorrow or will I get to stay with you?"

"I do not have to work tomorrow, Janine," Molly responded. "We will stay home tomorrow and you can play with Niles." Niles was a large cat that Molly had befriended and he now took up residence. He was fat as could be and had plenty of rats and mice to keep him that way, but he was also company for the two ladies in the small apartment.

Molly placed the coat on Janine and reached in her bag taking out a half of a loaf of fresh baked bread. She handed it to Mr. Roland and thanked him for the coal. He took the bread and smiled at Molly.

"The things you do for these children is thanks enough," Mr. Roland said, as he hugged her and Janine. "You two stay warm and we will see you on Thursday, Janine."

Janine smiled as she skipped out the door holding onto Molly's coat. As they walked down the sidewalk, Janine was full of questions as usual, but Molly had her eyes on the surroundings. She was aware of everything because it was important to be. There were people out on the streets that would like nothing more than to take advantage of a young woman and a small girl. It just wasn't safe. About a block from the apartment Molly observed a group of men standing near a fire barrel. As they approached the group of men one of them stepped away from the barrel and into the path of Molly and Janine.

The man appeared to be in his forties with a scraggly beard and dirt on his clothes and face. He half grinned and spoke in a raspy voice questioning Molly as to where she was going. Molly had stopped walking and Janine moved closer to her. Janine was not afraid but she did not like the man.

"We are headed home," Molly said, "now if you will kindly move aside we will be on our way."

"Well now," the man said, "wouldn't you like for me to walk you home? Then maybe you could fix me up some grub and we could have a little fun after you put the brat to bed."

"Mister," Molly responded, "I have no desire or intentions of fixing you a meal or taking you to my home. My husband would surely not appreciate it and I am sure he would tend to you properly." Molly let her hand be seen as the ring glittered from the fire light of the barrel.

"Well then missy," the man continued, "why don't you just take that ring from your finger and give it to me, then you and the brat can be on your way."

"Sir," Molly replied, "I have no intention of doing that either."

About that time Janine stepped up to the man and kicked him in the shin causing him to bend over and grab his leg.

"Why you little," the man started to speak but was interrupted by a strong burly voice.

"What seems to be the problem here?" questioned an officer sitting on a large horse.

The man looked up seeing the officer and immediately straightened up.

"Nothing officer," the man said.

Molly spoke up and said "well not exactly nothing Officer Barber, how are you this evening?"

"I am just fine, Molly." Officer Barber said, "What's this bloke been doing?"

"Well," Molly said "he just wanted to assist me to my apartment and use my ring for his own purposes. I have advised him that I did not share in his endeavor."

The man spoke quickly, "I didn't mean anything by it officer, I was just funning with the lady, that is all."

Officer Barber spoke in a very strong and loud voice, "Let me tell you something you street urchin, I should take your sorry hide to the brig. Instead, I am going to let you leave here and get out of my district. It ends at Jackson Square so if I see you east of there, I will put you in the brig just for walking on my street." "Do you understand me?"

A quick response came from the man, "yes sir officer, I will be heading out of here right now." None of the other men around the barrel moved and even snickered when the man grabbed up a sack of clothes and headed off down the street.

"He had that coming," one of the men said, "he was new to the area." "Tell you the truth officer we didn't like him anyway." The five men standing there then busted out in a song. The song was harmonized and it really sounded good.

"Thank you, Officer Barber," Molly said. "I don't know what would have happened if you hadn't of come along."

Janine had walked over to the horse and was rubbing him on the neck.

"How would you like a ride home lass," Officer Barber asked Janine.

"Really Mr. Barber," Janine said with excitement. "Can I Molly?"

"Of course you can," Molly said. "It would be nice to have Mr. Barber walk home with us."

Officer Barber stuck his hand down and grabbed Janine by the arm, swinging her up on the horse and placing her on the saddle in front of him.

"Okay lass," the officer said, "Apache is all yours, take the reign's and head us to your home."

Janine grabbed those reigns and they headed towards the apartment. Officer Barber and Molly talked as Janine lead the big sorrel to the front of the apartment. Officer Barber eased Janine to the ground and bid them good night, walking off into the darkness.

They entered the apartment and Molly was glad to be safe inside. She stoked a fire in the stove and fixed some homemade soup. The two ate and then Janine washed up for bed. After saying her prayers Molly tucked Janine into bed and kissed her on the forehead.

Molly walked over to the window and sat looking out at the street below. She could hear the street sounds and knew that it would be late before things quieted down. Sitting there she thought of home and how she would sit in the window and watch the river flowing by. This was such a change for her and she found out that it wasn't the life that she wanted to continue to live.

She asked herself how she could return home and carry

Janine with her. Had she shamed herself with anyone at home and what would she do when she saw Willie? Could she take up where she left off with him or was it too late? She hated to leave home the way she did, but she had too and no one would understand if she told them why she left. She missed Willie awfully, but it had been five years and she felt that things would be too late for her and Willie. She had listened to others talk about Willie and she was ashamed to tell people she knew him. Now she was older and she knew she had made a mistake in leaving. Willie would have taken care of her because she knew he loved her.

How would she explain that she had taken the ring to prove her love for him? She had put the ring on her finger when she reached New Orleans and she had not taken it off. People thought she was married and that was the way she wanted it. No man called on her so she didn't have to worry about men asking her out or wanting to date. Janine was another story for later. Mr. Roland had made sure that Molly got Janine whenever she wanted to and that both of them where taken care of. It was an understanding that Mr. Roland agreed to and he had been one of her best friends since she had been in New Orleans.

Now she was growing home sick. She missed the swamp and the river delta. She missed her family, and she missed Willie because she loved him. She didn't know when, but she was going home soon, and when she did she didn't care who knew how she felt. She wanted Willie in her life and she wasn't going to let life slip by her without being happy. These streets were bad for her and Janine. She would return home soon and make the life she had been wanting. She would return to her family and she would return to Willie.

There were things she needed to tell him. She just hoped that it wasn't too late. She prayed Willie would forgive her and love her as much as she did him.

Thursday came very fast and Molly dropped Janine off by the orphanage. She arrived at the bakery early, just as she had been doing for the past three years. As she tied the apron around her waist, Ms. Nan came from the kitchen. There was a heavy aroma of fresh bread being baked.

"Good morning my dear Molly." Ms. Nan said as she greeted her. Nan was a nick name of course, Ms. Nan's name was Nancy Gaelle, a short built woman of medium weight and a heart as big as the skies. She was also very good friends with Mr. Roland and gave all she could to the children at the orphanage. Her last name, which was French for a caring and giving person, fit her. On this day Molly noticed a strained look on Ms. Nan's face. It concerned Molly but she didn't ask what was wrong. She knew that Ms. Nan would tell her if she wanted too.

Near the end of Molly's shift, Nan walked up to her and said what Molly had expected.

"Molly," Nan started, "things are very slow and as much as I wish I didn't have too, I can't afford to keep you here any longer." "Business has been slow and this depression is making things so much worse." "I am truly sorry Molly, you are a very good worker and I hate having to do this."

Molly touched Nan on the arm and said, "now don't you be fretting over it Ms. Nan, I understand and I know that you have kept me here longer than you should have."

"I promise you that I will hire you back when things pick up," Nan said. "Just check in with me every day or so."

"Naw," Molly said, "I may come back one day Ms. Nan,

but I think I will use my money that I have saved and go home for a while." "I have been planning on it, just didn't want to leave you."

Nan reached into her apron pocket and handed Molly a week's pay and one day extra. "You keep in touch with me Molly, I will be worried about you," Nan said.

"I will Nan," Molly said, "and you be careful, there are some bad folks around here." Molly hugged Nan and thanked her for the opportunity to work there at the bakery. Molly then headed home and stopped by the orphanage to pick up Janine. After telling Mr. Roland what had happened, she told him she would be leaving New Orleans very soon and would take Janine with her.

"I couldn't think of anyone else she would be better with than you, Molly," Mr. Roland said. "You just make sure to take care of yourself and come back to see us." Molly hugged Mr. Roland thanked him again for everything.

"You have been such a good friend." Molly said. "Will you be able to give me paperwork on Janine in case anyone asks?"

"Why of course, Molly, When will you be leaving?" asked Mr. Roland.

"I am going to pick up the train tickets and leave for Mobile in two days," Molly said. "I will have my sister pick us up there. She has just finished college and is a doctor."

"It will be sad to see you leave Molly, and little Janine too," Roland said. "Promise me you will get these things straightened out. You know I will always keep your secret."

"I know you will, Mr. Roland," Molly said, I appreciate everything you have done for me."

Molly hugged Mr. Roland and turned to leave as Janine

came skipping through the door. Mr. Roland gave Molly some papers and hugged Janine. As they headed down the street, Molly was thinking about home and the things she had to do. She went by the train station and purchased two tickets for Mobile and then sent a telegram to Nicole letting her know when she would be arriving in Mobile. Nicole was working as an intern at a hospital there and went home on the weekends. Molly was scared but ready to return to the swamp. She needed to mend some fences and try to make things right. She slept very little the next two nights and was up early when it came time to catch the train. As Janine and Molly stepped onto the train and found their seat, Molly looked out of the window at the New Orleans skyline. She had been to the big city now it was time to go home to her family and the one man she missed the most, Willie. It would surely be a homecoming no one would forget.

Chapter 16

HOMECOMING IN THE SWAMP

Janine ran up and down the train car, greeting people and looking at the scenery along the rail as the train moved towards Mobile. After a few hours the conductor came by letting everyone know the next stop was Mobile and those getting off should gather their belongings. Molly grabbed the two suitcases from under the seat and held onto Janine's hand as the train came slowly to a stop at the depot. The two pieces of luggage were all Molly and Janine had to show for five years in the big city. They stepped off of the train and could hear Nicole yelling the minute they stepped onto the platform.

"Sis," Nicole yelled running down the platform at Molly. "I am so glad to see you."

Molly grabbed Nicole and gave her a big hug. "I am glad to be back," Molly said.

Nicole grabbed one of the suitcases and turned to walk down the ramp when Molly stopped her.

"Nicole," Molly exclaimed, "I am not alone."

Nicole turned around and noticed Molly holding the

hand of a little girl. The second Nicole saw her she paused and her face flushed. "Molly?" She said.

"This is Janine," Molly said, "she is from an orphanage in New Orleans."

Nicole had not moved but stood looking at the little girls hair and eyes. "She is beautiful Molly," Nicole said. "She looks like …"

"She is from an orphanage in New Orleans, Nicole," Molly said.

Nicole still looking at the little girl nodded, "Okay" she said. "Whatever you say Molly."

Nicole reached down and touched Janine's face saying, "Hi there, I am Nicole."

Janine looked at her and said, "I know Ms. Molly has told me everything about you. It is very nice to meet you, and you are so pretty"

"Well now that was very nice of you, I think we will get along just fine, Janine," Nicole said.

They headed down the ramp and to the car that Nicole had gotten for graduation. Janine was excited, she had seen plenty of cars but had never ridden in one. Everything was exciting to her and she already knew she liked this city better than she did the one she came from.

As they pulled out of the train depot, Molly grabbed Nicole by the arm and had her stop the car. To the right of the train station, was a loading dock and standing there were Willie and Sam, talking to Mr. Mercurio. Molly wanted to jump out of the car and run to Willie, but now was not the time. He had not seen her and for now she had others she needed to talk to and clear things up with before she spoke to Willie.

They pulled out and headed on down the road. Sam didn't tell Willie, but he saw Molly in the car. He wanted to say something but thought better of it. He knew Molly had seen Willie, but he didn't know who the little girl in the back seat was. The two men completed their deal with Mr. Mercurio and headed back towards Stockton in the truck.

Sam kept asking himself what was going to happen now that Molly was back. He didn't have a clue, but he hoped they could work things out. The past five years had been miserable for Willie. He had not gotten over Molly and spoke of her every day that Sam saw him. Willie's life had changed, and in a lot of ways Sam felt that Willie had given up on everything, especially himself. Willie had become pretty much a loner and never strayed too far from home. His only visitors were Sam and Cotton and the only reason they visited were to check up on Willie to make sure he was okay. The old bear Yam had left a year or so before probably moving deeper into the woods. Poachers had killed Two Toes, but they met the wrath of Willie when he caught them. No one was sure what became of them, but Sam had some ideas and they weren't good. The fellows were from north Mississippi and it was hoped they made it back to where ever they came. The only friend that Willie had and trusted was Bait. That damn dog was with Willie everywhere he went and would never be found to far from his side. Other than that Willie had pretty much become a hermit.

As they approached Stockton, Willie looked at Sam and asked, "Did you see her Sam?"

Sam felt like he was struck with a bag of bricks and said, "Who?"

"You know who, Sam," Willie said.

157

Sam felt like a kid caught with his hand in the cookie jar. "Yeah," Sam answered, "I was kinda hoping you didn't though. She don't look like she has changed much."

"No she didn't," Willie said. "She's still as pretty as she ever was."

"Well, what are you going to do?" Sam asked.

"I'm going to do what I have been doing," Willie said, "I am going to stay to myself and if she wants to talk to me she will. If not, then that is the way it is. I love her Sam, but ain't no need in me begging her to be with me. She left without much of a reason and I have hurt since she left. I can't go through more hurt."

"Well for your sake my friend," Sam said, "I hope things go the way you want. I will be here for you to talk to if you need me."

"I know you will Sam," Willie said. "You and old Bait are the ones I count on."

There was nothing else said the rest of the ride home. Sam could see the sadness in Willie's eyes. It wasn't a sadness because Molly was back, it was a sadness of not knowing what was to come and a sadness to know that more heartache might be on the way. Willie was a very strong man but Sam didn't think Willie could take much more hurt. No man could if he loved a woman like Willie loved Molly. Time would tell.

That afternoon Molly arrived home and she was so glad to be back. The reactions to Janine were all about the same as Nicole's but she immediately got into the swing with the family. Hunter had her helping him chase a couple of chickens for some chicken and dumplings on Sunday. It would be a homecoming. Hunter had married and built a house on ten acres near the Bell homestead. Other brothers, David and Charles had done the same. The youngest brother Jacob still lived at home, but was a big help to his maw and paw. Lisa had moved away when she married, but didn't live but a couple of miles away and stayed at the ranch as much as she did at her place. Her husband was a hard worker and logged for a living. He was gone more than he was home, but Lisa loved him dearly.

Janine acted like she always did, perky and happy, watching things going on and trying to do the things others did. She reacted with everyone and pretty soon had the whole Bell clan eating out of her hand.

Molly set a bed up in her old room that Janine could sleep on and Mrs. Bell helped. It was obvious that Mrs. Bell had questions and Molly knew it wouldn't take long before she started asking.

"Maw," Molly said as she set down on the edge of her bed, "I need to talk with you."

"I speck you do, Molly," Mrs. Bell said.

Molly spoke to her maw and both women cried and hugged each other for a long time. It was almost an hour before they came down from the room and began supper for the family.

"What you have told me will not leave my lips until the time is right, Molly," Mrs. Bell said, "but it is on you to seek Willie out and get things straight with him."

"I am, Maw," Molly assured her, "I just have to get the right time to do it."

"Time gets away from us, daughter," Mrs. Bell said, "don't ever know when things may change for the better or worse. I wouldn't put it off too long."

Molly smiled at her maw and nodded her head. It was good to be home and feel safe again back in the swamp. Her thoughts were of Willie and she longed to see him and try to explain things.

Sunday morning the family loaded up in the boat and headed to the First Baptist Church in Stockton. Everyone was happy to see Molly back home and they fell in love with Janine. The orphanage had taught Janine manners and she was polite with all the grown-ups. She played with all the children there and had them all playing games in the courtyard after the service.

On the way back to the dock Molly again saw Willie. He was headed toward Sam Burns, which was on the other side of town. She started to wave but didn't. Willie didn't stop but she knew he saw her. It was going to take some courage to speak to him, but she would, just not right now.

Willie slowed down as he passed the dock and was going to stop, but when he saw Molly, looking at him but making no indication that she wanted to talk to him he kept going. It was great to see her again but it hurt too. How long would it take to get over her? In five years he had not even gotten a letter or received any words from or about her. Now she was back and he had seen her twice yet she had not even acknowledged him. Willie felt that God knew this had to hurt and maybe them being together was not intended to happen. Willie wanted to hold her so badly no matter what had happened in the past. Every time Willie thought about her it hurt, but he would be patient and see what happened. It was all he could do.

After arriving at Sam's, Willie loaded the truck with some sugar and he and Sam headed off to the steel that was about twenty miles away. Sam's wife had come from church and all the talk was about Molly returning home and the little girl she had brought back with her. As Sam and Willie were driving through some back roads, Sam started to speak to Willie about what his wife had told him.

"Wife said Molly and a little girl she had with her was staying with the Bell's," Sam said.

"What little girl?" Willie asked.

"They say her name is Janine and she has dark red hair and dark eyes," Sam answered. "Sounds like she is full of energy and cute as a button. Wife says she looks to be around five years old and as smart as a whip."

"Why would she have a little girl with her Sam?" Willie asked.

"Says she is from an orphanage in New Orleans and Molly has adopted her," Sam said. "Seems like Molly was a little lonely and took a liking to this little girl. She showed them papers and all."

Willie looked confused and questioned, "Five years, huh?"

Sam answered, "That is what they said." Sam paused for a minute and looked over at Willie. "Willie, wasn't your maw's name Janine?" He already knew the answer, but wanted to see if Willie was paying attention.

"Yeah," Willie replied, "and she had dark red hair."

Sam knew exactly what Willie was thinking. Willie was looking straight ahead and now was not saying anything. They drove on and Sam couldn't help himself and asked Willie a question, "What you going to do now Willie?"

Willie looked at Sam asking, "What do you mean, Sam, what am I supposed to do?"

Sam thought a minute and said, "I think you should carry your ass over there and call her out on it."

"Sam," Willie responded, "it wouldn't solve anything. Molly has seen me twice and has not attempted to speak to me. Besides, she has papers showing she adopted the girl, we are just speculating. I am going to leave it alone."

"Well," Sam said, "I damn sure would, you need to know, Willie."

Willie looked at Sam saying "She has papers."

The sadness in Willie's heart swelled. Now, Molly had a little girl and from what he could hear the little girl was the right age and had similar traits and looks. He would like to know for sure where the little girl came from, but he swore not to call on Molly. If she wanted him to know she would tell him. Maybe the adoption papers were legal and she had found a little girl that looked like his maw.

The Bells had a big welcome home dinner for Molly and Janine. Food was all over the place and people from the church had been invited. Molly greeted everyone but she missed Willie. She wished she would have stopped him at the dock, but it was too late now. She would have enjoyed his company. She talked to all the people and even asked them about Willie. She got the same response from everyone. Willie had become a loner and was very seldom seen by anyone unless he had business in town. Seemed as if he had placed a wall around himself and most there said he seemed sad. They speculated that he had lost his maw and paw and then that gator had got killed and the bear up and left so that made him sad. Molly knew why he was sad and she knew she could change things, and she would very soon.

The next morning Nicole went to town and took Janine

with her. They were in Mr. Hymil's store to purchase some supplies when the door opened and Willie walked in. Nicole greeted him and Janine stood looking at him.

Willie smiled at the little girl even though inside he knew he didn't need any more reason or proof. He knew this was his little girl.

Nicole introduced Janine to Willie.

"Wow," Janine said, "you are a very big man."

Willie grinned and said, "Yes I am and you are a very small girl, how old are you?"

"I am five," Janine said, "Is that your dog?"

"Well I guess you could say that," Willie said. "He follows me around all the time, but he pretty much comes and goes as he pleases."

"What is his name?" Janine asked.

"His name is Bait," Willie said.

Bait walked up to Janine and was wagging his tail and licking her on the hand.

"Well now that is strange," Willie exclaimed, "he doesn't usually come to strangers. He must like you."

Janine giggled and lost her attention on Willie while playing with Bait. Nicole had stood back and listened to the conversation without saying anything.

"It is time for us to leave Janine" Nicole said.

"Yes ma'am," Janine said as she looked back at Willie. "You have a very nice day, Mr. Willie."

"I will," Willie said, "and you have a nice day too."

Nicole quickly rushed Janine out the door and they headed back home.

"That was a very nice man," Janine said.

Not knowing what to say Nicole just nodded.

Willie walked out of the store and back towards his truck. A tear was stuck in the corner of his eye. He reached up and touched it with his finger and watched the boat leave the dock with Nicole and Janine. Janine turned and waved at Willie and he raised his hand to wave good bye. He then turned and lowered his head as he got into the truck and headed back home. The small child had reminded Willie of so many things, some good and some bad. Her eyes and hair was that of his mother and he could see it as clear as day. If Molly had adopted this child then she had selected one that reminded him of the only other woman that had ever been in his life. The only thing was, Molly had never met his maw and didn't know what she looked like. Seeing the girl stirred up questions and memories. Willie felt that it was meant to be and even though it made him sad, he was happy to have met Janine and hoped to get to talk with her again. If only Molly would talk with him, if only she loved him as he did her. These were his dreams and he felt nothing would come of them. These were his thoughts and that was the whole point. These were things he wished for, but it did not seem that Molly wanted the same things.

Chapter 17

SADNESS ON THE DELTA

It was an early spring morning and Molly had been home two weeks or longer. On this morning she had made up her mind, she was going to see Willie and hoped that he would understand why she had left. For the first time in a long while she was happy. Today she was going to let Willie know her true feelings and she didn't care what anyone thought. She climbed into the boat and shoved off from the bank.

Willie had gotten up early and left before dawn. He was going to run his trot lines and limb lines. After he finished, he had made up his mind to go see Molly. He was down emotionally, and he just had to know how she felt. He talked to Bait all the way to the lines in Hastie Lake. The morning was calm and warm and Willie found the fish to be in a mood to eat. As he rounded the bend of the creek, he saw the gypsy wagon sitting near the edge of the embankment. The gypsy, Tasha, motioned for Willie so he slowed the boat and cut off the engine.

"How are you today?" asked Willie.

The gypsy had a look of concern on her face as she

answered him, "The day is beautiful only to the eye, but Willie it has trouble in it. I have seen you and know that you are sad and even though I am not supposed to try and change fate, I would ask that you return home just for today."

"Now ma'am, I appreciate your concern but I have obligations to fulfill and I am old enough to take care of myself," Willie said.

"I told you I would return one day, Mr. Cane," Tasha said. "I would not have done this for anyone but you. You have had a very hard life, but things can change for you if you will just let this day pass."

"Again, I appreciate your concern ma'am," Willie said as he leaned over to pick up a line from the bottom of the boat. He looked back up at the embankment and the gypsy was gone. Now he wasn't one to be afraid of much, but this gypsy put a fear in him. He shook his head and looked at Bait. "I got to stop smelling that shine I been making."

Willie thought about the warning and continued to run his lines. His thoughts were of Molly and if anything the gypsy said was true, it was that he was sad. He had to get over these feelings and the only way was to see Molly and get things settled. Willie cranked the motor up and headed down the lake to finish checking his lines.

Near the end of the lake Willie reached over to grab a limb line, and before he could react a big cotton mouth moccasin grabbed him on the forearm and filled him with venom. Willie yelled and jerked the snake out of his arm. While Willie still had the snake it struck him again hitting his leg. Bait came off of the seat of the boat and grabbed that snake about mid body. The snake then turned on Bait and bit him behind the neck. Willie finally grabbed the snake and threw him out of the boat.

Willie knew it was bad, he had been struck twice and Bait once. Cotton Mouths were the meanest and most poisonous snakes in the swamp and their bites were deadly. Willie had been attacked by humans and animals, surviving all of them but this time he knew he was in trouble. He cranked the boat and headed for the houseboat some six miles up the river.

In what seemed like hours Willie finally made it to the houseboat. He picked Bait up out of the boat and staggered to the door. The poison was beginning to take its effect and he was finding it hard to breath. He laid Bait down by the door and the dog just looked and him and tried to wag his tail. Willie rubbed him on the head as old Bait convulsed with foam coming out of his mouth. Then just like that Bait was gone.

Willie cried and stood up and instead of getting in the truck and trying to get to Doc. Bettner, he walked in and took the box out from under a board near the wall. He set the box on the table and sat down to write a letter. He was shaking and the pain was almost unbearable, but Willie knew he would not make it to the doctor. He looked up and in the door stood Tasha.

"Are you ready, Willie?" she asked.

He looked up and shook his head saying "In a minute, need to write this." He now knew who the gypsy was and why she was there.

Willie took the pencil and scratched out a letter on a piece of paper,

It read "My Dearest Molly, I am sorry I have to leave

this way. Deep inside I felt that you really loved me and didn't want to leave me. I don't really know if I could handle things if you didn't so in a way I guess this was the best way for me to go out. The box has everything that I have and I leave it to you and Janine, the little girl you brought home. I hope it will help. Remember until your dying day Molly, I loved you as no other could or ever will. I will be waiting for you at the gate if the Lord lets me sit there. Love Willie."

Willie laid the letter in the box and leaned his head back on the rocking chair. As he closed his eyes he realized that he didn't hurt and then he heard Tasha call him again.

"It is time, Willie," Tasha said. "You will see her again before you know it."

He stood up and followed Tasha into a light that seemed very bright and beside him was Bait.

Sam and Cotton came up the dirt road to get Willie to help them dig up some stumps. As they pulled up Sam saw the door open and Bait laying by it.

"Something is wrong, Cotton," Sam said. "Bait is always right by Willie, something ain't right."

They walked over the gang plank and onto the porch. Sam looked down at Bait and then rushed into the door. He stopped in his tracks and said, "Willie, oh my friend, Willie, why didn't you get some help."

Cotton bowed his head and said, "He could have stopped at the wharf, he passed right by the Doc's office. Doc Bettner could have helped him 'stead of that poison killing him like that."

Sam just stood looking at Willie with his head back on the chair and said, "Wasn't the poison that killed him Cotton, Willie Cane died of a broken heart. Nothing else in this swamp could have killed him, but a love he had in his heart."

They picked Willie up and laid him on his bed and Cotton brought Bait in and laid him at the foot of the bed.

Sam sent Cotton to get the Sheriff and Doctor Bettner, since Doc was the only coroner in the north end of Baldwin County. As soon as Cotton got out of site Sam sat on the porch and saw a boat coming up the river.

Molly stepped on the porch of the houseboat and Sam stood up.

"Hello, Sam," Molly said with a smile on her face. "Where is Willie?"

Sam took Molly by the arm and said, "You need to sit down Molly, I'm afraid I have some bad news for you."

"What is it Sam, where is Willie?" asked Molly as her voice began to get louder. Molly broke loose from Sam and went through the door with Sam trying to stop her. As she entered the room she saw Willie laying on the bed and Bait on the bed at his feet.

"Oh my God! No!" Molly cried as she fell to her knees. "Why Sam, why was he taken from me? I was coming to tell him everything and I was going to be his wife, why did he leave me?"

Sam took her and started to lead her away, but she moved away from him and walked over to Willie. She leaned over and kissed him. "I love you, Willie Cane, and I always have. I will not be with another. I will come to you Willie, I will come to you," Molly said as she wept.

Sam finally got Molly to leave the room and closed the door. He then handed her the box and showed her where Willie kept it. She took it and read the letter that Willie had left. The Sheriff and Doctor Bettner arrived, and soon they carried Willie away.

Molly went to town and made the arrangements for his funeral. He would be buried at Jug Lake with his mom and dad. He would also have his one true companion Bait buried at his feet.

Molly made it back home very late and her mom and Nicole were sitting there waiting. They saw the sadness in her eyes and knew that there would be no sleep for her, at least not on this night.

Molly rocked and cried most of the night. Nicole set with her and tried to comfort her, but nothing she could say would help.

"I should have been with him, Nicole," Molly said, "He should have known everything, especially that I loved him. He deserved to know and I let him down, he deserved to be loved by me and I let others tell me what to do. He should still be alive with me, and us as a family."

Nicole didn't know how to respond. She could only sit there and hold her sister and try to comfort her.

"I am sure he knew, Molly," Nicole said. "He knew you loved him, the letter even said that he felt that you did. I know this can't be easy for you, but you have to think about Janine, she needs you right now too."

Molly thought for a moment and said, "Yes she does and I will take care of her the way I know Willie would have taken care of both of us."

Molly finally went to sleep late into the night, but was up early. Everything was as a dream, and she was numb. Her feelings had left her and she didn't have any more tears to shed. She had made a promise that she would keep and no matter what she would keep it. She would never let anyone take Willie's place.

The day of the funeral the whole town gathered. Willie Cane was a legend in the community and everyone knew him. He never hurt any man that treated him or other people fair, and he would give you anything he had if you needed it. He was the best trapper and guide in the Tensaw River Delta Swamp and treated everyone equal. He was feared, but for some reason everyone trusted him. It was no secret about his love for Molly and everyone knew he would have married her. He would be missed by Sam, his one true friend. Buried by the willow tree, facing east, Willie would be able to watch the sun rise every morning over the swamp that he was the king of. At his feet would be his canine friend, Bait.

Over the next three years Molly withdrew into a shell to the point that no one could cheer her up. She refused any help from anyone and would often be found at the old houseboat just sitting on the porch. Janine was raised pretty much by Lacy and Nicole, each teaching her how to do things around the house. Molly had lost interest in everything but Janine and spent every moment with her that she could, but still Janine being there wasn't enough to make Molly happy. The only thing that Molly ever spoke about was Willie and how she had let him down.

After three years of torturing herself, Molly just gave up. She died and was buried beside Willie on Jug Lake. On the day of the funeral Janine was kneeling near the grave after some of the people left.

As she stood there a lady walked up behind her and

said, "Hello Janine," my name is Tasha. "I just wanted you to know that Molly is happy now."

Janine looked back at the woman with her pretty black hair and olive complexion.

"How do you know that?" Janine asked.

"Because I have ways and you will soon understand why she is happy," Tasha said.

"You will see a new world and you will understand why things have happened as they did. You take care of yourself, Janine."

Janine stood up and turned around, but the lady was gone. Mrs. Bell walked up and asked Janine who she was talking too.

"I don't know, Mrs. Bell," Janine said. "A lady just told me that I would understand everything and then she was gone."

Mrs. Bell looked around and saw no one but said to Janine, "I have to tell you some things. You asked me why we buried Molly here by Willie Cane. Well the truth is that Willie Cane and Molly are your parents. Your maw left the swamp and moved to New Orleans when she found out you were going to be born. She was afraid that she would bring shame to the family. I told her we could work through anything, but she said she had to leave. I knew the first day I saw you that you were the daughter of Willie. So Janine, you are the daughter of one of the most famous men to ever come from around here. I am your grandmother and you are the daughter of Willie Cane and Molly Bell."

Janine grabbed her grandmother and hugged her and they both stood there crying. This was just the beginning for Janine.

Chapter 18

ALL IN A NAME

Janine learned the ways of the swamp, and how to take care of people through her work with her Aunt Nicole. Her grandma had taught her to cook and sew and she went to school and got an education. She missed Molly a lot and hated that she never knew that Molly was her mother until after she died. She felt the same about Willie, but she had only spoken to him once. She wondered many times what he was like and hearing people talk about him really excited her. Everyone knew she was the daughter of Willie Cane and Molly Bell and no one looked down on her. She was accepted.

At almost seventeen, Janine was called into her grandma Bell's bedroom. Mrs. Bell was sick and wanted Janine to have something. Janine entered the room and Grandma Bell was sitting up in the bed. She patted the edge of the bed and indicated that she wanted Janine to sit down.

"How are you feeling, Grandma?" questioned Janine.

"I have had better days my child, but I need to take care

of something before the good Lord sends someone for me," said Mrs. Bell.

"What?" Janine asked.

Mrs. Bell took a leather pouch off of the night stand. She opened it and took a folded letter out and handed it to Janine.

"Your mother wanted me to give this to you right after she died but I held on to it because I wanted to be able to teach you how to take care of yourself," Grandma Bell said. "I think it is time because you know how and what to do in life and I feel that you will probably be around this swamp until you die."

"What is in the letter, Grandma?" Janine asked.

"I don't know child, it was left for you and that is the way it should be," Mrs. Bell said. "Now you run on and help your Aunt Nicole, I am going to take a nap."

That night after supper Janine went to her room and took the letter out of the pouch. She read it and found out that her mother loved Willie very much and that if he had not of died they would have been a family. Molly spoke in the letter about Willie's kindness and how he cared for people. She said that Willie had left some things for her and he left a drawing showing where the stuff was in the old houseboat. Molly explained that those things would now belong to Janine as she was the rightful heir of Willie Cane and Molly Bell and that her true birth name was Janine Cane.

The letter told about New Orleans and the people there, and how and why they had helped Molly. Everything that Janine had ever questioned in her mind was in the letter. It was something that Janine would hold onto forever.

The next morning Janine made her way to the old houseboat. As she neared the old houseboat, it looked to have sunk on one end. The gang plank leading to the porch was very unsteady and kudzu vines had made their way onto the houseboat and taken over the roof. Janine eased her way across the gang plank and could feel every step as the houseboat moved under her feet. She opened the door very slowly and jumped back as two baby raccoons came running out the door past her. It shook her up, but she continued into the room. The right side of the boat was sitting down in the water but the left side was dry. She looked around the room and could see that it had her maws touch.

Things in the room had been placed there by Molly while she grieved and would spend hours alone there. An old place mat was lying near the table and Janine had seen it before. It was one that her mother had made from twined horsehair. Janine took out the instructions and made her way to the wall near the left side of the cabin. At the side of the fireplace she saw the initials WC carved on a board plank with a knot hole in it. The board was recessed in, not the same size as the others.

She pulled the board back by placing her finger in the hole and sliding it. As she did, she found the wooden cedar box and pulled it out of the space where it had been carefully placed. On top of the box was carved "Molly and Me". Janine felt at ease in the cabin but wasn't sure if it would sink with her inside, so she made her way off of the old boat and headed home. Just as she was leaving she looked back at the old houseboat and heard a pop.

The boat was held in place by two large ropes that had deteriorated by the elements. The pop was one of the ropes snapping and the houseboat tilted back against the other rope. Within a matter of a minute the second rope popped and the old boat eased down into the water of Briar Lake, completely submerged. It was as if those old ropes knew that they had to hold until Janine could get that box. It was now serene and the lake didn't have a ripple on it as if Willie Cane had been waiting for that moment and was now finally at rest.

When Janine got home she showed her Aunt Nicole the box and they sat down at the kitchen table. As Janine opened it a tear came to her eye as she saw a hand printed note that said, "Goodbye Janine, Willie and I will see you in heaven." Her mother had known about the box and what was in it, but she never tried to use it.

After removing the note Janine found the wedding rings and the diamond ring that Molly had used in New Orleans. There was a deed to twenty-five acres of land on Tensaw Lake and about thirty thousand dollars in cash-but that wasn't all. Nicole gasped when Janine pulled out forty or more bonds that had been saved from before the turn of the century. There were for the G&O Railroad and Walter Cane had started collecting them before he died.

"Janine, do you know what those are?" asked Nicole.

"No ma'am," Janine responded, "What are they?"

"Those are bonds and they could be worth a lot of money." Nicole said. "Take them to the bank tomorrow and see Mr. Dunn. I will go with you, because having those could be dangerous."

"Why, Aunt Nicole?" asked Janine.

"Things are hard on people now and if anyone knew you had those they may try to rob you of them and that money. Don't tell anyone you have them and we will get you to the bank in Bay Minette to see Mr. Dunn. He is the bank's president and he can take care of them for you," Nicole said.

The next morning Nicole carried Janine to the bank and they met with Mr. Dunn in his office. Mr. Dunn made several calls and within an hour they had an account set up for Janine.

"We will take care of your money," Mr. Dunn told Janine, "and you can get what you need when you need it." As he was explaining things to Janine and Nicole he received a phone call. He was speaking when he half stood and looked at Janine. "You are sure," he asked the person on the other end of the telephone. "Okay," was all he said as he hung up the phone.

"Miss Cane, he said, the bonds you found are worth more than I expected," said Mr. Dunn.

"What are they worth Mr. Dunn?" asked Nicole, "a couple a thousand dollars?"

"No Ms. Bell," said Mr. Dunn. He sat back down and punched in numbers on his calculator. "Janine," he said, "you are now worth one million seven hundred and thirty five thousand dollars."

Janine's mouth fell open and Nicole just set staring at Mr. Dunn.

"With your permission I will handle the finances of the bonds and make sure you get every penny earned or you can let the bonds build, but I am not sure the G&O will be in business much longer," said Mr. Dunn.

Nicole was the doctor of the family and she had been doing business with Mr. Dunn for a long while.

"I trust you, Mr. Dunn," Janine said. "You take care of it for me and thank you."

As they walked out of the bank both Nicole and Janine seemed to be in shock. It was something not expected. The thirty thousand in cash would have taken good care of Janine, but now she was a millionaire in a part of the country where there weren't many.

"Well Janine," Nicole asked, "what would you like to do for the rest of the day?"

"Let's go shopping, Aunt Nicole," Janine said, "I feel like it might be fun for once in my life.

Both the ladies let out a hoot and headed towards Mobile.

Janine became known very well in the town of Stockton and helped her family. She ended up marring a young man named Corey Burns, the son of Sam Burns, Willie's best friend. They purchased two hundred acres of land near Dennis Creek and raised four children. All of the children graduated from college and were successful in business. Janine started a wildlife game reserve and used the twenty five acres on the Tensaw as a starting point for an animal clinic to help injured wildlife in the area. Corey had a lumber company which grew quickly and he was soon the top lumber man in the southeast.

After the children had left home, Janine and Corey purchased a house in New Orleans as a vacation home. While there, Janine visited with Mr. Roland who was now in his eighties and still had all his faculties. He remembered Molly especially, and how she came to him and asked for help while carrying Janine. He had agreed to say that Janine was an orphan, but made Molly promise that she would tell everyone someday that Janine was her daughter.

In all Janine had a good life, and it was all because

she had a mother and dad that cared. Janine never felt like she could do enough to keep their names alive. Janine had learned well from Grandma Bell and her Aunt Nicole on how to bake. With that knowledge she purchased the old bakery that Molly had worked in. Before she knew it, Janine had opened seven more bakeries from Pensacola to Baton Rouge.

As Corey and Janine walked down the streets of New Orleans she said, "You know, we have everything we want and even though my family is gone, I can still feel them both near. I couldn't ask for anything else Corey, I am the daughter of a famous swamp man and a mother who loved me enough to protect me from ridicule."

They stopped in front of the old bakery and looked up at the sign that was over the front of it. In large letters was the name Cane's Bakery, and in the lower right hand corner in small print, In memory of Willie and Molly Cane. In the door was a sign that read "Today's Special, Swamp Fritters". Janine smiled at Corey as she unlocked the door and said, "I have a last name, I am the daughter of Willie Cane."

Across the street stood a gypsy lady with shoulder length black hair. She smiled.

The End

Eddie J. Carr

Printed in the United States
By Bookmasters